"S

v

say it.

"Why don't you tell me?" she threw back at him, "since you claim to know the reason."

"Money," he said coldly. "What other reason? You've run up some debts for yourself and you suddenly remembered the very rich Holden Greystone that you once knew. And to what lengths are you prepared to go to get your hands on a bit of my money?"

Marie found her voice at last. "How dare you!"

"You have a child, Holden," she said in such a low voice he had to lean forward to hear. "A daughter. She's ill with leukemia. She needs an operation, a bone marrow transplant. You're her only chance. That's why I'm here."

CATHY WILLIAMS is Trinidadian and was brought up on the twin islands of Trinidad and Tobago. She was awarded a scholarship to study in Britain, and went to Exeter University in 1975 to continue her studies into the great loves of her life: languages and literature. It was there that Cathy met her husband, Richard. Since they married, Cathy has lived in England, originally in the Thames Valley but now in the Midlands. Cathy and Richard have three small daughters.

Don't miss *Secretary on Demand*
by Cathy Williams
on sale in August, Harlequin Presents #2270

Books by Cathy Williams

HARLEQUIN PRESENTS®
2222—MERGER BY MATRIMONY

Don't miss any of our special offers. Write to us at the following address for information on our newest releases.

Harlequin Reader Service
U.S.: 3010 Walden Ave., P.O. Box 1325, Buffalo, NY 14269
Canadian: P.O. Box 609, Fort Erie, Ont. L2A 5X3

A Burning Passion

CATHY WILLIAMS

THE MILLIONAIRES

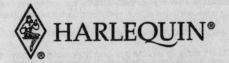

HARLEQUIN®

TORONTO • NEW YORK • LONDON
AMSTERDAM • PARIS • SYDNEY • HAMBURG
STOCKHOLM • ATHENS • TOKYO • MILAN • MADRID
PRAGUE • WARSAW • BUDAPEST • AUCKLAND

ISBN 0-373-80518-7

A BURNING PASSION

First North American Publication 2002.

CHAPTER ONE

It was two o'clock in the afternoon, and right now, right here, Marie could not imagine being anywhere more absolutely perfect, short of heaven.

She had only been on the liner for a matter of days, but she had already slipped into that blissful, relaxed frame of mind that always seemed to be the by-product of an abundance of warm sun, blue skies and marvellous food. And of course sea. Lots of it.

She stood on the deck, in her regimented uniform of yellow Bermuda shorts and grey T-shirt with its discreet GH insignia on the pocket, and squinted against the sun at the dazzling blue water with its ribbon of white foam which the liner was leaving behind. She had always loved the sea. The Cornish coastline where she had spent her childhood had remained with her even after her parents had died and she had, seven long years previously, moved away to live with a distant relative in London. It was in her blood. She could understand how people became fascinated with its endless changing moods and were tempted to throw everything to the winds and flee the grind of daily existence on a boat headed nowhere and everywhere.

It had been a stroke of unimaginable luck to have landed this job aboard the *Greystone H*. She had been sick to death of London, even sicker to death of her aunt who had never made her feel welcome in her neat, precise little terraced house, and ripe to take the first escape route possible before she threw herself on to the mercies of the job market.

Thinking back on it, she had no idea how she had managed to persuade the agency that she was right for the job on board the liner. She had no experience of waitressing, which was what she would be doing, albeit on a slightly more erratic schedule than in a conventional restaurant. She had even less experience of working on the high seas, despite having been surrounded by the grey Cornish ocean for fourteen years. In fact, it had only occurred to her during the interview that she might well turn out to be horrifyingly seasick the minute the liner left port, a fear which, fortunately, appeared to have been unfounded. She was twenty-one years old without a great deal of useful experience in anything, and she had been stunned when she had been informed that they had accepted her application.

'You should have got something better paid and local,' her aunt had said with her usual brand of good cheer. 'What's the point in taking time off before you look for a job? Four years at university was time off enough, if you ask me. Do you imagine that we don't need the money? This little break is hardly a paying proposition, is it? I would have thought that you might have seen your way to helping me out a little financially, considering I have spent the past four years at your beck and call.'

Marie had tried not to look too staggered at that one. The art of debate was not one in which her aunt indulged, and she had learnt from very early on that it was far better to preserve a tactful silence on even the most outrageous of her aunt's statements, because her aunt never ventured opinions. She stated, and she never expected contradiction.

'You can have whatever I earn on the liner,' Marie had said truthfully, because, for all her aunt's faults, she had taken her in when her parents had died, and she had allowed her to pursue her education, even though she had regularly punctuated her niece's final two years at university with constant unhelpful reminders that there were far too many graduates in the world, that what she needed were some practical skills instead of an English degree, which would get her precisely nowhere when it came to landing a job.

'I wouldn't dream of it,' her aunt had sniffed. 'I dare say you will put it aside, however, for a rainy day? I needn't tell you that life is full of rainy days.'

All in all, it had not been as rough a ride as Marie had anticipated. They had parted, temporarily, with a sense of relief on both sides and a brief peck on respective cheeks, and now here she was, out in the blue yonder, with a balmy breeze blowing her ponytail across her shoulders and the warm sun toasting her face to a nice golden colour. And in return for this slice of heaven, not to mention freedom, all she had to do was serve tea in the main dining-room at three-thirty, help behind the bar in the evening, and generally make herself useful in the kitchens.

She spent another half-hour on the deck, chatting with some of the guests, most of whom recognised her by now, and then she headed back to the dining area.

The liner was the last word in luxury. It had been saved from an ignominious demise in a company which had been going downhill for several years by a speculator, an enormously wealthy speculator, who had bought it, renovated it and, in the space of only a few months, had turned it into a profitable concern. Marie had gleaned all of this from various members of the crew, who had all worked on the ship in its sad, declining days, and were

full of praise for the man who had spared them the dole
queue. Since he had also, in a manner of speaking, given
her a break from her aunt, and a wonderful breathing
space before she waded into the job market, she was quite
happy to nurture warm feelings towards this faceless
stranger as well, with his sharp eye for a bargain and
enough loose cash to turn it into reality.

The dining area was only half-full. Quite a few people
were napping in their cabins and the rest were scattered
throughout the ship, soaking up the sunshine next to the
swimming-pool, or snoozing on the deck, or playing cards
or reading in the large, comfortable lounge area which
had been furnished to give the impression of being a home
away from home. A very expensive and plush home away
from home.

Tea in the dining-room consisted of tempting cream
cakes, guaranteed to add a few pounds before even the
first bite was taken, pots of coffee and an assortment of
teas, quite a few of which Marie had never even heard of
before she had come to work on the liner. Fruity teas,
speciality teas from the Far East, as well as the usual
English varieties. Like everything else, it was all something of an eye-opener.

As a child, she had been raised on good, solid, old-
fashioned English cooking, and her aunt had continued in
the tradition with rather more of an emphasis on small
portions. She was a great believer in 'waste not, want not',
and Marie had grown accustomed to eating every mouthful of what was presented to her, whether she liked it or
not.

University at least had given her some respite, but not
much, since she had continued to live with her aunt for
financial reasons, and her aunt had made it patently clear

that whatever freedom university life offered ceased very firmly at her little red front door.

Here on the *Greystone H* she was constantly amazed at the huge wastage of food. Even after all the guests had been fed, and the crew had taken their fair share, there was always something to be discarded. If she ever came into contact with the Wealthy Speculator, as he had been nicknamed in her mind, maybe she would point that little element of wastage out to him.

Things were buzzing in the kitchens. The chefs were already preparing some of the dishes for that evening, and the cakes were all laid out, ready to feed the masses.

Jessica, one of the girls of similar age to her own, who also worked on the catering side, looked at Marie with a good-humoured grimace and poked a finger into her own stomach.

'What does this look like to you?' she asked, and Marie eyed the area thoughtfully.

'Well,' she said with a straight face, 'I never was all that good at biology, but I'd hazard a guess that it's your stomach.'

'Ha ha. It's not just my stomach. It's my fat stomach, it's a stomach that can't resist all these concoctions, it's a stomach with a mind of its own.'

She handed a tray of cakes to Marie to take out to the buffet table.

'How am I ever going to manage when I come to running my own catering business if I end up eating all the food?' she wailed, and Marie grinned.

'You'll manage,' she said. 'You might be fat but you'll still be efficient.'

They giggled together, and trundled out with their trays. Jessica was still chatting, and Marie listened, chipping in every now and again. By nature she was a reserved girl,

quite shy in company, a legacy, she suspected, of her
background. Here on the liner, though, there was no room
for shyness. The crew had accepted her like an old friend,
with the affinity of people who shared each other's lives
practically twenty-four hours a day. It was team spirit
such as Marie had never experienced before. As an only
child of elderly parents she had been happy, gloriously
happy, but quite solitary and rather sheltered, content to
play by herself; and living with her aunt had done nothing
to change that. She had had her school friends, of course,
and later her university friends, but a childhood spent re-
lying on only herself for companionship had taught her a
measure of self-control which was now an ingrained part
of her personality. While her friends threw away their
dolls in favour of the opposite sex, Marie had quietly
watched from the sidelines, never participating in the
headlong rush to discover her sexuality.

All that, she thought vaguely, would come in time.
With her corn-blonde straight hair, her widely spaced
brown eyes, her neat, regular features, she had attracted
her fair quota of boys but she was in no hurry to enter
into the roller-coaster game of dating, despite the friendly
persuasion of her peers.

In fact—and this was something which she would never
have admitted in a thousand years—the boys she had met
at university had done nothing at all for her. They were
ordinary. They didn't inspire, and love, when it hit her,
would be wonderful, inspiring, a firework display. All
those things which her aunt had steadfastly warned her
against over the years. Dark and dangerous, to Marie's
untouched mind, did not threaten, they beckoned. Why
sell herself short for anything less?

The sprawling oak sideboard with its crisp white linen

tablecloth was now groaning under the weight of cakes, crockery, serviettes, jugs of fruit juices, glasses.

The dining-room had filled up and people began trickling across to help themselves to the various assorted delights. At the end of their three-week cruise most of them would return to their homes several pounds heavier, but right now thoughts of that were very far from their minds. They were well and truly submerged in that holiday mentality that said eat now, diet later.

Marie began going round her appointed tables, chatting with the guests and taking their orders for tea or coffee. When she had first started she had found this quite confusing, had had to concentrate on getting the orders right, but now it was like second nature, not least because the same people invariably sat at the same tables and ordered the same things. Even on holiday people could be tremendously predictable.

'Shall I make this really interesting for you and order a gin and tonic?' a voice said from behind her. It was a deep voice, with just enough of a lazy, amused drawl to it to send the colour rushing into her face. She spun around and opened her mouth to explain, as politely as possible of course, that alcoholic drinks were not encouraged outside bar hours, but the words stuck somewhere in her throat. Rather like her brain, which seemed to have suffered a similar paralysis.

She was staring up at the most impressively handsome man she had ever seen in her life. He had grey-blue eyes, the colour of the sea in winter, and thick black lashes which made them appear sexy rather than forbidding. His hair was as black as his lashes, and his features were aggressive rather than beautiful. His whole bearing spoke of power. Even with no real experience of men, Marie could sense this instinctively. He was the sort of man who attracted stares. He was attracting them now. Perfectly coiffed middle-aged ladies, elderly ones with grey hair, looked at him surreptitiously as they strolled back to their tables with their china plates and glasses of fresh juice.

Marie realised that she was gaping and she shut her mouth abruptly.

'I'm afraid we do prefer our guests to defer their consumption of hard alcohol until a little later when the bar opens.'

'Is that a fact?' There was the same undercurrent of amusement threading this question and he continued to stare at her until she felt compelled to break the silence.

'We do offer a selection of teas,' she said, licking her lips, 'also coffees, juices…'

'You do, do you? And is that all you have to offer?'

Was he flirting? She was beginning to feel hot and bothered, and she tried to think back to what had been said on the subject of guests who might get it into their heads to make passes.

'If you'd care to tell me which is your table, I would be happy to bring you a menu card with the full range of beverages,' she said.

'How thoughtful of you.' He smiled at her and there was something electric about that smile that made her pulses begin to race.

This sort of reaction to a man was not one that she had experienced before, and a gut reaction warned her that it was dangerous, that this man was dangerous. She felt a terrible jolt of illicit excitement.

He moved away towards one of the tables and she watched his loose-limbed, graceful stride, fascinated. He sat down and crooked a finger in her direction, and she walked across to where he was sitting.

'I'll have a pot of tea,' he said, 'for two.'

'Oh, yes, of course.' She lowered her eyes and felt a sharp, unpleasant tug of disappointment shoot through her. So he was with someone. That made sense. He had not struck her as the sort of man who travels alone, nor did he strike her as the sort of man who ever ran short of female companionship.

'You have a most transparent face,' he said casually, fixing her with those incredible grey-blue eyes. 'I can see the thoughts flitting across it. How old are you? Seventeen, eighteen?'

'Twenty-one. And I really can't stay and chat to you.' She glanced behind her to where Jessica caught her eye meaningfully.

'Twenty-one? Odd.'

'What's odd?'

'Most women by the age of twenty-one are blasé to the point of cynicism, but you're still a blank page waiting to be written on. Am I right?'

Another wave of heated colour surged over her. This was a level of banter which was way out of her league. She felt like a mouse being played with by a cat for its own personal amusement.

'I've never given it much thought,' she said stiffly, embarrassed. 'Now, if you'll excuse me.' She turned around and walked towards the kitchens, aware of his eyes on her.

Jessica grabbed her the minute she passed through the swing door.

'Who is he?' she asked. 'Where did he appear from? He wasn't here last night. I'd have noticed.'

'I have no idea who he is,' Marie answered, not caring for the wave of confusion that swept over her when she thought of that hard-boned, amused face.

'Didn't he say? You and he seemed to be spending

rather a lot of time chatting. He must have told you his name.'

'Nope.' She braced herself to walk back into the dining-room with some of her orders, and Jessica followed in her wake, giving full vent to her curiosity.

'The man with no name,' she murmured dreamily. 'Romantic.'

'He's a guest,' Marie reminded her. 'And a guest with another half.'

'Ah. So you two were getting to know one another.' She shrugged. 'Well, good luck to whoever's caught him.'

He was still sitting at the table and it took a conscious effort of will not to look in his direction. He made her feel gauche. True, she was gauche, but she had always managed to hide that under a façade of self-composure. This man, though, addled her without trying, and that she found slightly alarming. It was a relief, in a way, that he was with someone, that he was a guest on board the ship and she was a waitress, with strict rules about fraternisation.

She found that she was perspiring slightly when she returned to the kitchens for her tray, this time with cups of hot chocolate for a youngish couple on honeymoon, both of whom were Mormons and forbidden to indulge in caffeine.

When she returned to the dining-room it was a shock to see that the man's guest, his companion, his whatever, was not long and blonde, which was what she had expected, but a mature woman, in her fifties at least, despite the autocratic good looks and the pampered elegance.

He caught her eye and shot her a half-smile, which she pretended not to notice.

When she took the pot of tea across to them, she couldn't meet his eyes.

'I don't believe I know your name,' he said smoothly, as she rested the pot on the table.

'Marie Stephens, sir.' She still wasn't looking at him, at least not directly, and her smile was polite and glassy without being offensive.

'Marie Stephens Sir,' he said thoughtfully. 'Unusual name.'

She did look at him then, annoyed to be the butt of his amusement in front of the woman sitting next to him and now eyeing her with cool courtesy.

'Darling,' she said, resting her hand on his arm, 'leave the child alone. I doubt she can handle your sense of humour.'

The woman looked at Marie, not exactly with dislike, but with the bored, patronising expression that some very wealthy people cultivated towards their less wealthy counterparts. She was attractive, and in her day must have been quite something. Her blonde hair was a bit faded, but it was perfectly styled and still thick. Her eyes were blue and assessing, her bone-structure classical.

'I'm sure I can,' Marie replied, trying not to show her irritation with this sweeping statement. 'I am paid, after all, to handle most things aboard this liner, including a sense of humour which I may not find particularly funny.'

'I don't think I care for that tone of voice one bit, my girl,' the woman said, without emphasis yet still managing to endow her words with a great deal of meaning, and Marie forced herself to look apologetic. That was another thing she had been told when she had landed this job. The customer was always, always right, even when he or she was wrong.

'I'm so sorry,' she said in a low voice. She wasn't looking at the man at her side, but she knew that his eyes were on her. She could feel them. It was like being touched.

The woman waved her hand dismissively in a gesture which suggested that it should never happen again, and Marie breathed an inward sigh of relief. This job was precious to her and she wasn't about to jeopardise it because one of the guests had taken an instant dislike to her.

'Will there by anything else?' she asked politely, and the woman turned to the man and said, 'Holden, is that all for you?'

Holden. Unusual name. His long body was relaxed in the plush pink and burgundy chair, his fingers lightly clasped together. He had long fingers and strong arms, sprinkled with dark hair which curled around the gold band on his wristwatch. He was looking at them both lazily, amused, spectator at an entertaining cabaret being performed for his own personal benefit.

'Oh, yes,' he said, 'for the moment. But,' he added, glancing at Marie sideways from under those thick, black lashes, 'don't stray too far.'

Don't stray too far? Marie smiled politely at him and thought that she intended to stray as far as she possibly could.

She kept very far away from his table until the tea things were being cleared away, then, out of the corner of her eye, she saw his companion get up and move away, her walk slow but elegant, the gait of someone who expected the world to make way for her, and the chances were it probably did.

What did he see in her? Marie wondered. He looked the sort of man who could have anyone. Maybe it was her money. Money, she assumed, could be a powerful magnet. Having never had it herself, she found that concept a little difficult to comprehend, but she had seen enough of the way her friends had spoken about their boyfriends in varying degrees of awe depending on what car they drove, or what clothes they wore, to realise that the toys that money could buy spoke volumes. And money didn't just buy toys, did it? It bought people as well.

He was still sitting at the table when all the other guests had finally filed away. Marie glanced across at him from beneath lowered lashes and felt another silly shiver of awareness. Who was he? What was his relationship to the woman? She hated to find herself speculating like this, and in fact it was the first time she had done so since she had started work on the liner, despite the fact that there were an awful lot of people around her and their accumulated fortunes could probably have kept the crew in food and clothes for the rest of their lives. The other members of the crew played guessing games when it came to the guests, wondering aloud what each did for a living, sketching imaginary scenarios about them, and Marie usually just listened while they spoke, giggling occasionally at their conclusions.

Now to find herself feverishly wondering about a complete stranger confused her. Jessica, she knew, twenty-one going on thirty-five, would have had no trouble in handling a man like him, but she, Marie, was more like twenty-one going on sixteen, and as pure as the driven snow. Too many books and too little experience, she had once been told acidly by a rejected suitor at university, had turned her into an innocent living in a glass box. He had made her sound like a freak, but she still preferred the glass box to a bed with a man she didn't love.

When she saw him beckoning her across, she took a deep breath and made herself remember that this job meant a lot to her, a lot more than the casual interest of a passing stranger with whom, anyway, a relationship was forbidden by company rules.

'Yes?' she said shortly, standing in front of him, then she had to force her features into something resembling a friendly smile. 'What can I do for you?'

He gave her a long, assessing stare, his lips curving into a devastating smile. 'Hard, isn't it?' he murmured.

She said, not following, 'What is?'

'Being polite to someone whose sense of humour you find tedious and not very funny.' He said that as though he really didn't mind, as though the thought of it was quite amusing, in fact.

'I apologise if that's the impression I gave.' That took quite a bit of effort because she didn't feel at all apologetic. She felt disturbed and taken aback. She could feel herself beginning to fidget and she clasped her hands together in front of her.

'Sit.'

'I'm afraid I can't. Socialising with the passengers isn't encouraged.'

'According to…whom?'

'According to the people who employed me.'

'In that case, they can deal with me if they don't like it.' He wasn't a man who expected his orders to be disobeyed. She could tell that easily enough from the tone of his voice, his cool sense of command.

Marie hesitated and sat down, but she couldn't resist one nervous glance behind her to make sure that her boss, Henry, wasn't in the process of storming up on her from behind.

'You needn't worry,' Holden said easily, 'nothing's going to happen to you if you chat to me for fifteen minutes. Are you always this jumpy?'

'Are you normally this bossy?' she said by way of response, and he grinned.

'All the time.'

'In that case I feel sorry for the people who work for you.' She had no idea why she said that, since she didn't have a clue what this man did for a living, but instinct told her that if it involved other people, then he would not be one of the ones taking the orders.

'What a relief my teatime companion isn't here,' he drawled. 'She definitely would have taken offence at that.'

'And I suppose you listen to everything she says?' Marie with horror heard herself ask. If she didn't watch it she would soon be crossing that fine line between having a job and being out of work. What was it about this man? she wondered.

'I try to,' he murmured, looking at her carefully. 'There are very few people I defer to, and she's one of them.'

Because she pays the bills? Marie wanted to ask. Are you her kept man? She found the thought of that so distasteful that she looked away.

'I see,' she said instead, crossing her ankles, then uncrossing them, then crossing them again.

'Oh, dear,' he murmured softly, 'you think that I'm her gigolo, and you find that idea very disturbing. Why? The world is full of women who sit back and live off their husband's earnings without the slightest qualm in the world. Why should it be different when the tables are reversed?'

She looked into those peculiarly light, watchful eyes with their mesmerising sensuous gleam, and felt as if she were drowning.

'It's different, because...because it just is.'

'What inescapable logic.'

She stood up, flushed. 'I can see it's really making your

day needling me, but I'm not about to stand around and tolerate any more of it. I realise that you're a passenger on board this ship, but that doesn't give you the right to insult me.'

'Oh, sit back down. No one's insulting you.' He looked warmly amused at her outburst.

'I really must go and help out in the kitchens, anyway,' Marie said, hovering indecisively, and he frowned with a hint of impatience.

'Take it from me, you won't be reprimanded for talking to me.'

'Not even by your teatime companion?' she asked sweetly, sitting back down but still feeling uncomfortable despite his reassurances.

'Oh, yes,' Holden said seriously, 'perhaps by her. Yes, definitely by her. My mother is relentlessly predictable in her choice of the women she feels are suitable for me.'

'Your *mother*?'

He raised his eyebrows as if surprised that she might think otherwise, but there was a trace of mockery in his eyes.

'Of course, who else? Oh, yes, I forgot, you thought that I might have been her toy boy.'

Marie went bright red. She felt confused and unruddered by this man. The self-control on which she had come to rely over the years, even to expect, had deserted her in one fell swoop and, every time she tried to recapture it, it seemed to float away just out of reach, leaving her defenceless.

'I didn't think that at all,' she lied, looking at him then quickly lowering her eyes.

'No,' he said thoughtfully, 'of course you didn't. What are you doing tonight?'

'I beg your pardon?'

'Tonight. I expect you have to help out in the kitchens over dinner, but what are you doing afterwards?'

'Afterwards? Nothing, I guess. I thought I might watch the cabaret show from backstage. Quite a well-known comedian is going to be performing.'

'Join me on the deck.'

'I really don't think so.' Alarm bells were really ringing in her head now. Marie had no objections to getting involved with a man, but this man was way out of her league. He had said it all when he told her that she was the sort of girl of whom his mother would heartily disapprove. Still, a thread of excitement fluttered through her, and a new and strange sensation made her pulses begin to race.

'Why not?' he asked bluntly. 'I promise to keep my hands to myself.'

That made her blush even harder, and she couldn't think of a thing to say.

'I really mustn't,' she stammered into the silence. 'I could lose my job if...'

'I'm talking about a chat on the deck, not sex.'

'Yes, I know,' she replied, clearing her throat and trying to sound more composed that she felt, 'it's just that...'

'I know, I know.' He looked at her intently. 'If you like, you can consider it an order from your boss.'

'What are you talking about?' She raised bewildered eyes to his.

'I'm your boss,' he explained patiently. 'I'm Holden Greystone and I own all this.'

'You're not, are you?' she asked, and he nodded. 'But if you were, are...everyone would have recognised you.'

'Why would they? This is the first time they will have seen me and, on my orders, the captain is keeping quiet about my identity. I want to see how things are run without the drawback of people knowing who I am.'

'But that's not fair!' Marie protested, and he shot her an ironic look.

'When it comes to business,' he said, 'it's very fair indeed. Employees have an annoying tendency to alter their behaviour if they know they're being observed by the boss. So I don't want you to gossip behind my back about what I've just told you. I flew in last night, landed by helicopter with my mother and as far as everyone is concerned, apart from a handful of people, I'm no more than a late arrival, delayed for a few days because of illness in the family. That way I can see at first hand how efficient the crew are.'

'Then why are you telling me all this?' Marie asked, perplexed.

'Because—' his voice was low and husky '—I like you. I want to get to know you better, and if I'm to do that, you've got to stop thinking that every time I look in your direction you're going to get into trouble.'

'But your mother...'

'When it comes to women, my mother thinks she can run my life, but of course she can't.' He was smiling, but his voice was flat and hard, and she could see how formidable he could be given the right circumstances. Not a man to cross.

She thought that everything, this conversation, Holden Greystone, all of it had a dreamlike quality about it, as if any moment she would open her eyes and discover that she had been imagining the whole thing. She knew that when it came to men she was unbelievably inexperienced, but she had not yet realised just how inexperienced she was. Until now.

*   *   *

Later, standing outside on the deck, which was deserted because the passengers were one and all in the Show Room, being entertained by some extremely funny risqué jokes, it dawned on her that what she was doing here was treading water. At the moment she was happily keeping afloat, but if she wasn't careful she might find herself drowning without any lifebelt to cling to.

Holden Greystone was frighteningly intelligent, self-confident, witty.

She looked at him surreptitiously. Against the starry, warm night, his profile was etched against the horizon. Just at that instant he turned to her and their eyes tangled. Marie felt her heart begin to pound. What was he thinking? What was going through that head of his? His hooded eyes gave nothing away and she found, with nervous, dry panic, that she couldn't stop staring at him. She hadn't drunk a thing but she felt as though she had consumed several bottles of champagne which had gone to her head, muddling her thoughts, sending reason out of the window.

She couldn't remember what she had talked to him about for the past hour, even though she knew that she had talked a lot, more than she ever had with anyone in her entire life. He drew conversation out of her, made her feel at ease, yet horribly excited and wary at the same time. She was feeling distinctly excited and wary right now.

He reached out and stroked the side of her face with one finger, a tender, teasing touch that sent the blood rushing to her head.

'I want to kiss you,' he said, 'badly, but I won't if you don't want me to.'

She could hear the sea lapping against the side of the ship as it glided through the black water. The air was soft and dark like velvet and only the slightest of breezes rustled through her hair, lifting it gently off her shoulders. It was difficult to think that inside there were over two hundred passengers, talking, chatting, drinking. Out here, it was as if only the two of them existed in the entire universe.

Her breathing was quick and, as his head swooped down to hers and his lips met hers, a small groan escaped. She raised her arms, linking them behind his head, allowing him to pull her towards him so that her body moulded against his. She kissed him feverishly, passionately, shuddering as his hand stroked the curves of her body.

'You're beautiful,' he muttered against her neck, and a thrill of recklessness ran through her like a bolt of lightning. 'Exquisite. I've never met anyone like you in my life before.'

He cupped her breasts with his hands and stroked them, until she wanted to scream with desire.

Her body was untouched by any man, a blank page on which all experience was yet to be written, and against all common sense she had an overwhelming longing that this man be the one to do it.

He drew her back and said softly, 'Not here. Not like this.' He was smiling. 'When I take you I want it to be memorable. I don't want you ever to forget, because I know I won't.'

They walked back into the ship in silence, but a companionable one, and she had the sensation of being on the brink of something, perhaps of discovering herself.

'The ship docks tomorrow in Grenada,' he murmured. 'We'll have a bite to eat at one of the restaurants. We'll talk.' They were standing outside the main entrance to the lounge, where people had congregated around the bar area. Through the paned glass, they seemed unreal.

He kissed her on her forehead and smiled down at her.

'You're like a gazelle,' he said softly. 'I don't want you to run away.'

Then he was gone and she remained where she was, breathing in the stars, the moon, the bottomless black sea.

Are you the tiger? she asked herself. Should I be afraid? And if you're dangerous, how can danger be so tantalising?

CHAPTER TWO

AFTER her parents died, Marie used to have one recurring dream. It was of falling. Of course, she always woke up before she had actually touched ground, but the impact of the dream had nevertheless always been frightening. She used to lie in bed, reliving that nightmarish feeling of being weirdly out of control, hurtling towards oblivion.

Now, in Holden's company, she found that that sensation of falling was with her once again, though not in her dreams. It was there every time their eyes met, and her heart skipped a beat whenever he touched her, and her skin grew hot and sensitive, even though he had made no effort to do anything beyond kissing.

The liner had docked in Grenada two days ago. The passengers had streamed off clutching their straw hats, their suntan lotions, heading for the market, then for one of the more popular beaches, where they could soak up the sun before returning to the air-conditioned comfort of the ship.

It had been a bit awkward evading Jessica, who had wanted to follow the troop to the market and buy some local souvenirs with her, but she had managed it, and she and Holden had taken off to one of the less well-known beaches.

She stood still in the middle of the restaurant kitchens with a smile on her face as she recalled how much they had talked. She could remember the conversation, every

word of it, in surprising detail. She could also remember
the feel of his fingers linked through hers, the amusement
in his eyes as she skipped along the nearly deserted beach,
loving the soft, white sand under her feet. She had pranced
around, turning circles, laughing, and he had stood there,
his sensuous mouth curved into a smile, watching her.

The warm sun, the swaying palm trees, the turquoise
sea were not a novelty to him. He had, he had informed
her, been to the Caribbean several times, but she had
never been. She had never even thought of going in her
wildest childish imaginings. Her parents would never have
been able to afford such luxury. Her holidays had been to
rented cottages, mostly in the Lake District, and twice
they had gone to Brittany.

Grenada, with its sweet smell and pristine beaches, was
paradise. She could have walked along the beach forever
without getting bored, and thinking back on it he had been
an integral part of that excitement.

She could hardly believe that she had been so uninhib-
ited and carefree in his company. She had almost forgotten what it was like to let her hair down and be a child.

Jessica brought her back down to earth. Her arms were
laden with plates and she whispered under her breath,
'Whatever planet you're on, you'd better come back down
to planet *Greystone H* double quick, or Henry's going to
serve you up for dinner. What the hell are you daydreaming about anyway?'

'I wasn't daydreaming,' Marie replied, wiping her
hands on her skirt and then moving on to collect her orders.

'Oh, no?' Jessica called out after her, raising her voice
above the general din in the kitchens. 'Was that a spot of
transcendental meditation you were practising, then?' She

laughed loudly at her own joke and Marie grinned from
behind her.

'Of course it was,' she said gaily, 'very relaxing.'

Holden wasn't in the dining-room. He was having dinner in the captain's private quarters. His mother was
seated at her usual table, however, and Marie glanced over
at her warily. She had had no further confrontations with
the older woman, but that didn't mean that the well-bred,
watchful hostility was no longer there, because it was.
Marie saw it every time their eyes accidentally met.

She spent the better part of two hours serving, running
between the tables and the kitchens, her controls on full
automatic even though her mind was busily analysing everything that had happened to her over the past few days,
ever since Holden had arrived on the scene. She was still
enjoying herself aboard the ship, but that innocent enjoyment was now tinged with an edge of expectation. She
felt as though she were living in a permanent state of high
excitement and the novelty of the situation had dulled her
usually careful, guarded nature.

Most of the passengers were beginning to drift off.
Coffee had been served and drunk, chocolates had been
distributed, the cabaret in the main Show Room was about
to begin. This was the nicest part of the evening, the time
when she felt she could begin unwinding. By ten-thirty
she would be free to stroll around the deck.

She was smiling at the prospect of that, along with the
prospect of seeing Holden, who had arranged to meet her
outside in one hour's time, when she looked up and did
the one thing she had been studiously avoiding doing for
the entire evening. She caught Mrs Greystone's eye. The
older woman beckoned her across and Marie tried not to
look too dismayed as she approached her.

As usual, she was impeccably dressed. Marie doubted

that she had anything in her wardrobe that approximated to the kind of casual clothing which most normal women were wont to wear. Even when she was relaxing, Mrs Greystone's clothes spoke of tailored opulence. Now she was dressed in a coffee-coloured two-piece outfit and several strands of pearls with matching earrings. She looked elegant, attractive and very faintly intimidating.

Marie forced herself to smile and said, 'Good evening. Is there anything I can do for you? Some more coffee perhaps?'

'I have already had my quota of one cup,' Mrs Greystone informed her. 'Any more and I would have trouble going to sleep.'

Marie relaxed. The ice was still in the eyes but at least the conversation was harmless.

'We do provide some excellent decaffeinated coffee,' she offered, and then proceeded to reel off the various brands. Mrs Greystone looked at her without blinking.

'No, my dear, I don't think so. I abhor decaffeinated coffee, just as I abhor instant coffee. Tastes of nothing.'

Marie hovered.

'You've been seeing something of my son, I understand.'

Of course this was what it was all about. Mrs Greystone was hardly going to summon her across for something as innocuous as a cup of coffee, was she?

'Occasionally,' she murmured vaguely.

'Hardly that,' Mrs Greystone pointed out in a stony voice. 'I gather you have been spending a considerable amount of time together. Whenever you have a spare moment, in effect. I don't think that that is such a good idea, do you?'

'What do you mean?'

'I think you know exactly what I mean, my dear girl.'

Mrs Greystone surveyed her icily. 'Do correct me if I'm wrong, but you do not move in the same circles as my son, and we both know that while that does not matter on board a ship, it would matter a great deal should this relationship, for want of a better word, be allowed to continue beyond the confines of this.' She made a sweeping gesture around her but her eyes didn't leave Marie's face.

Marie looked down. She badly wanted to point out that that was something her son should decide for himself, but to do so would have certainly breached the bounds of courteous behaviour and would land her in trouble, so she kept silent and bit back the words.

'There is nothing I can do about my son seeing you, but I should just like to point out that this is little more than a brief holiday romance. I do hope you won't find yourself taking any of it too seriously?'

It was phrased as a question but it was a warning. Marie recognised that instantly. Mrs Greystone wanted the best for her son and she, Marie, did not by any stretch of the imagination fit into that category.

'The cabaret is about to begin,' she said politely. 'Are you quite sure that I can't bring you something? Tea? Or perhaps something stronger? We stock quite a variety of dessert wines and liqueurs.'

Mrs Greystone rose to her feet. It was only when she moved that her age became apparent, because her movements were so slow and unhurried.

She inclined her head, waiting until Marie had finished, then she said, 'I do hope you will think about what I have said, my dear girl. We wouldn't wish to be foolish over this, would we?'

Marie watched the slowly departing back with a mixture of nervous dread and muted panic. Part of her was also angry that she had been effectively pulled to bits and dismissed because of her background, but another part of her, that part which she had so successfully quelled over the past few days, could see the reason behind the warning.

Holiday romances were quite the norm on these cruises. She had been told that often enough by various members of the crew. The enforced intimacy played havoc with common sense and it was not unheard of for marriages to run aground before the ship had docked at the final port.

She was waiting for Holden less than one hour later, at their agreed place on the deserted deck. She had had time to have a quick shower and had changed into a pair of jeans and a red checked shirt which was very comfortable but made her feel a little like a cowgirl.

'Very fetching.'

She heard his voice before she saw him, and spun around, already smiling. It was a moonlit night and the silvery light threw the arrogant lines of his face into disturbing shadow.

We wouldn't want to be foolish about this, would we?

His mother's words flew into her head. He was so frighteningly handsome, she thought. Not a man ever to run short of female companionship. So what was he doing with her, apart from amusing himself within the confines of the ship?

That was such a disagreeable thought that she quickly pushed it aside. Lately she was finding it extremely easy to push aside her disagreeable thoughts.

'I feel as though I should be milking cows or chopping wood,' she said, walking up to him, staring up into his eyes and feeling that familiar little shiver of excitement.

He laughed, his eyes on her face, then touched her neck with his finger, trailing a path upwards to her ear, then coiling his long fingers into her hair.

'What a thought! I can't picture you doing either. You haven't got the build for it.'

'You have,' she pointed out, leaning against him and liking it as he slipped his arm around her waist, holding her so that they were both looking out towards the sea. 'I can't imagine you doing it either, though.'

'I pass on the cows,' he murmured, 'but I have chopped the occasional log or two in my lifetime.'

'Have you?' She sounded surprised and he laughed again with amusement.

'Oh, yes. I'm not completely removed from everyday life.'

'I never said you were.'

'You don't have to. As I said, your face gives a great deal away.'

'I'm not sure I like that.' She frowned slightly.

'It's a compliment. A lot of women would die for that youthful, appealing charm.'

'Tell me where you learned to chop wood.' She didn't want to dwell on what sort of women he had in mind. That would bring her too dangerously close to thinking about the sort of women he went out with, the sort of women his mother approved of. Her mind raced up towards that imaginary conversation and then skittered away. Here and now was not the place to face reality, not just yet.

'Canada,' he said, surprising her again. 'I spent one very cold, very snowy winter over there, in a log cabin by one of the smaller lakes in the north. It was damned freezing, and if I hadn't quickly got to grips with chopping wood I would very quickly have died of hypothermia.'

'What were you doing there?'

'Putting the finishing touches to the thesis I was working on.'

'Very adventurous.'

'It seemed a good idea at the time. I was tired of London. I needed to get away and that was perfect. The cabin belonged to a friend who only used it in the summer. He thought I was off my rocker.' He gave a chuckle.

'It must have been wonderful,' Marie said dreamily. 'Out there in the middle of nowhere with only nature for company.'

'And the odd bear. I fought them off with my bare hands.' He leant down to brush her hair with his lips and she laughed. She had never known anyone who could make her laugh the way he could. He had a dry, incisive humour that made her forget to protect her emotions.

'What a terrifying experience for the odd bear,' she said, when she had finished laughing.

'No doubt.'

'Have you been back there since?'

He shook his head slowly. 'Never had the time. I got caught up in the concrete jungle and then before I knew it I was thirty-three and log cabins seemed like a long time ago.'

'Shame.'

'Your heart bleeds, does it?' He laughed again, but as his hand stroked her back, there was an element of something else in his deep laughter, something sensual and arousing.

'Sort of,' she admitted. 'Concrete jungles sound like concrete cages. Don't you ever feel trapped?'

He gave her an odd look. 'Of course not. Why should I? What's the point of moving unless you move forward? Ambition is the lubricant that oils the wheels of life.'

'Surely not! Is money that important? I don't believe it is.'

He shrugged. 'You're the first woman I've ever heard say that.'

She laughed and wondered if that was a compliment of sorts. 'And I've never met anyone like you either, sir! Although, to be fair, university isn't the place to meet hungry, ambitious men. My friends, on the whole—' she wrinkled her nose '—tended to be a little broke. Ambition for most of them was stretching their grants out to last the term.' She laughed, but there was a serious element to her laughter. 'Most people, believe it or not, live modest lives and are happy just to get by saving up for life's little luxuries.'

'I have nothing against that,' he said a little coolly, but his voice implied that he was viewing it from a distance, a spectator but never a participant.

'I don't suppose you have any idea what it's like to be on the wrong side of the tracks,' Marie said with dry speculation, and he shook his head with mock sadness.

'If I'd known you were there, I might have jumped across to find out,' he commented with a grin, and she smiled back at him.

'You might have long legs,' she joked, 'but I doubt they could have spanned the distance between two worlds.'

'Oh, yes,' he murmured lazily, 'we're worlds apart. But that's what makes you the breath of fresh air that you are.'

'Poor little rich boy,' she murmured, holding the collar of his shirt with her fingers and looking up at him. She felt so alive. How could a whole lifetime have passed without her ever being aware that this drug existed? This powerful pull of attraction that could knock her sideways?

'I've never been called that before. No one would have dared.' He bent to kiss her lips and she thought that that was probably quite true. Holden Greystone was not a man to attract anything but awe. It amazed her that she was so relaxed with him that it was easy to pull his leg and it amazed her even more that he accepted it all with such easy amusement.

'A brief holiday romance.' 'We wouldn't want to be foolish about this, would we?' 'Breath of fresh air... worlds apart.' Something disturbing fluttered like a dark wind inside her.

The light touch of his lips deepened and his tongue thrust into her mouth, awakening an agonising need in her that radiated out from the pit of her stomach.

'I'm getting very frustrated,' he said roughly, and she felt a quiver of rising excitement at the huskiness of his voice.

'So am I,' she said frankly.

'I own this damned ship,' he muttered. 'I have half a mind to suspend you from further duty so that you can spend the time with me.'

'That would be a very bad idea,' Marie said, laughing. Because, she thought, what would happen to me after you'd gone?

'In that case, tomorrow when this ship docks at Martinique you and I are going to vanish for the day. That's an order.'

'And who am I to disobey?' She shuddered as his hand curved round the swell of her breast. She had not worn a bra and he unbuttoned the top three buttons of her shirt, then slipped his hand underneath to caress her warm, bare skin, rubbing the nub of her nipple with his thumb.

He groaned against her neck, and she could feel his

hard arousal pressing against her. Then he removed his hand and redid the buttons with unsteady fingers.

It shocked her to think that it was the last thing she wanted him to do, even though she knew that they could hardly make love out here on the deck, under the velvet sky and pale silver moon. She didn't like to think what her aunt would make of this behaviour. Sex was a topic that had never been broached between them, but Marie had always felt that as far as her aunt was concerned it was something vaguely unpleasant. There was nothing vaguely unpleasant about what she was feeling, though.

'I should let you run along to your bed, I suppose,' he muttered, 'now that our allotted time is probably up. I promised to meet my mother in the Show Room before she retires.' He sighed deeply and she had an insane desire to pull him back to her, to prolong the magic of the moment.

'Of course,' she said dutifully.

'Don't say it like that. Have you no idea with whom I'd rather spend the remainder of the night?'

That brought a smile to her lips and he pulled her back to him, kissing her hard, hungrily.

'Tomorrow,' he murmured. 'I'll meet you outside the ship at ten-thirty.'

She nodded and they strolled back along the deck before diverging, she to her room, he to the Show Room.

The thoughts crowded into her head the minute she was back in her room. She lay down on the tiny narrow bed and stared upwards at the ceiling, with her fingers clasped behind her head. Her body still ached from where he had touched her, so much but not enough. It was crazy. She had never behaved like this in her life before, had never felt like this. She was calm, controlled, one of life's observers. How could her personality have undergone such

an intense, radical change in less than a week? She wanted
to think coherently about it all, she knew that she had to,
but it was difficult. It was like trying to think intellectual
thoughts while riding a rollercoaster.

She slept in fits and starts, waking early to watch the
morning sun beginning its slow, burning ascent against
the horizon. She watched it through her little glass pane,
and of course it delayed her so that she had to rush about
madly in order to be in the kitchens in time for breakfast
preparations. Most of the people she worked with suspected that something was going on between herself and
Holden, but they didn't know her well enough to tease
her and, since it didn't affect her work at all, were prepared to live and let live, even though they must have
been puzzled as to why no one higher up the ladder had
seen fit to reprimand her for taking too much of an interest
in a passenger.

Only Jessica issued her with a word of warning, telling
her that it was all right for the plebs, as she affectionately
referred to her co-workers, to suspect dark and dastardly
things, but that she should be careful that no one more
senior found out.

No one more senior? Marie had thought with a dry
smile. All orders stopped at Holden Greystone.

Still, there was no way that she was about to take advantage of that, so she had wisely agreed, and really had
been so discreet that she wondered whether her true call-
ing didn't lie with the Secret Service.

Breakfast was uneventful. The passengers were excited.
Some of them had invested in small French dictionaries
and Marie overheard snatches of conversation being con-
ducted in laborious French over the croissants and toast,
which made her smile.

She wondered whether Holden's mother would be get-

ting off the ship. She assumed so, and she tried to picture
the expression on her face when her son informed her that
his day was otherwise occupied. It was not an agreeable
line of thought.

She headed back to her room to change as soon as she
feasibly could, slipping on her bikini, over which she
wore a thin cotton dress. Everything else she dumped into
her lightweight cloth bag which she slung over her shoulder.

Holden was waiting for her outside. She stood on the
deck of the ship and stared down, unobserved, at him. His
hands were thrust into his pockets, and his short-sleeved
shirt and shorts were a pale foil for his now bronzed skin
and lean, rangy body. He was wearing a cap, a faded blue
and green one, and from where she was standing he
looked every inch the manual worker, his body toughened
from the outdoors, every muscle honed to hard perfection.
No one would have guessed that this man controlled a
fortune that ran into millions, bought and sold companies
with an expertise that spoke of brains, talent and power.

She walked down towards the waterfront and he looked
up at her, their eyes meeting across the throng of people
disembarking.

It was a brilliantly hot day. The skies were clear and
blue, with the sort of hard colour that often accompanied
bitterly cold winter days in England.

The majority of the passengers were going to stroll
around the capital, absorbing the French atmosphere about
which they had received ample exalted description via a
short video which had been played for them the previous
day, and no doubt practising their French, which Marie
suspected might well prove to be an amusing source of
confusion for the native islanders.

The ship had docked for two nights. There was, the

enthusiastic voice on the film had informed them, a wealth of things to see. There were rain forests, lush and dark and wildly tropical, and there were beaches, and then there was the architecture, quite different from that of the rest of the Caribbean.

Marie vaguely thought that in normal circumstances she would be dying to cram it all in. Normal circumstances, however, had ceased to exist and now all she could think of as she walked towards Holden was that she was going to be spending the day with him.

'Waiting for anyone in particular?' she asked, smiling up at him, and his lips curved into a returning smile.

'No one in particular,' he said, in his deep, sexy voice, 'but now that you've come along, perhaps you'd care to join me for the day?'

'I have no objections.'

There was an electric undercurrent between them, a mutual awareness that was almost unbearable.

She followed him to the car which he had rented for the day, a blue Peugeot which looked only just on the respectable side of reliable.

'Where are we going?' she asked, settling into the passenger seat, and wriggling slightly because it was so hot from standing in the sun. She rolled down the glass quickly and turned to face him.

'Heading south,' he said, starting the engine, which spluttered into life, reluctant to be roused from its warm, cosy slumber. 'I've been doing my background research and there are a couple of isolated beaches there which we could explore.'

'Doing research?' Marie asked with incredulity. 'You mean you haven't been to Martinique before?'

'Never.'

'And you say that you're well-travelled?'

He grinned and glanced across at her from under his lashes. 'Appalling, isn't it?'

'Appalling,' she agreed, settling back against the seat and transferring her attention to the scenery flashing past them. She was getting used to the extravagant colours of the Caribbean, to the vibrancy of the flora. It was already becoming difficult to remember the grey monotone of London.

He reached out and placed his hand on her thigh, running it up and down, then he said matter-of-factly, 'I like your body. It's very smooth, very supple, as I imagine a ballet dancer's would be like. Have you ever danced?'

'No, never.' She laughed, liking the feel of his hand stroking her. 'In fact, apart from an occasional game of squash, I'm rather lazy.'

'Makes a pleasant change from all the diet-conscious, body-conscious women I've met in my lifetime.'

He returned his hand to the steering-wheel, and Marie asked in a controlled voice, 'Where's your mother today?'

'What an odd question. Does she intimidate you?' he asked, and she shrugged.

'A little,' she admitted. 'She thinks...'

'I know what she thinks. Believe me,' he said shortly, 'she hasn't been reticent on the subject of you. She has a natural aversion to any hint that a woman might be after me for my money. Can you blame her? I'm very wealthy and a wealthy man is often fair game for a certain breed of woman.' His voice hardened and there was enough cold ruthlessness in it to make her shiver.

'Money has got a certain amount of appeal, I suppose,' Marie agreed vaguely, and he looked at her, coldly unsmiling.

'Quite. But I don't care for gold-diggers, and any woman who sees me as a passport to the easy life is playing a dangerous game. But you're not like that, are you, my darling?' It was a question that masked a warning, and she looked at him, startled.

'Of course not.'

'Good.' He smiled and the dark threat receded. 'I should hate to be disillusioned.'

He refocused his eyes on the road, and when she spoke she tried to keep her voice light, even though what he had said had shaken her.

'I only asked about your mother because I would feel bad depriving her of your company.'

Holden flicked her a sideways look. 'As a matter of fact, my mother has had quite a bit more of my company than she had originally expected. I was only supposed literally to alight on the ship, check out how the staff were shaping up, and then leave.'

'Why are you still here, then?'

'Why do you think?' His voice was husky and she felt colour creep into her cheeks.

They were pulling up to the beach and, as he had said, it was deserted. On this sunny, windless day there was no one to disturb the tranquillity.

She hopped out of the car, breathing in the salt of the sea, slinging her bag over her shoulder, and he followed her after a while, putting his arm around her shoulder, and she linked her fingers through his. It was so peaceful. They strolled along the beach until they came to a clump of coconut trees, where he laid down his towel. He pulled off his shirt, then his shorts, to his swimming trunks underneath and she looked at his body, fascinated.

'Now you,' he said, grinning at her, and with slightly more self-conscious movements she stripped off her dress to the bikini.

'Swim?' he asked, and she shook her head.

'I think I'll just lie down for a while.'

'Only one towel.' He gave her a rueful look. 'We'll have to share.'

It was a huge towel, but not so huge that his body didn't touch hers when he lay down next to her, propping himself up on one elbow to look at her.

'It's gorgeous here, isn't it?' she asked.

'Gorgeous,' he murmured, his grey-blue eyes on hers. 'This is the first time we've been totally away from crowds. No familiar faces waiting to pop up just when you least expect it.'

'Yes.' She paused. 'There are a few raised eyebrows on the ship,' she said. 'Some of the people I work with.'

He shrugged. 'Does that bother you?'

'It would if it began to get in the way of my working relationship with them,' she said slowly.

He gave her a blank look, and she continued wryly, 'I can see you don't understand.'

'Of course I understand,' he said, resting his hand on her waist, then running it along her thigh. 'What kind of boss would that make me, if I didn't cultivate a good relationship with the people who work for me? I wouldn't let the opinions of other people dictate my actions, however. There's no room for that in the cut-throat world I live in.'

'What a trusting little soul you are,' she murmured, raising her finger to his lips, and he caught her hand between his.

'Do you realise you occupy an almost unique position in being able to pass comments like that?'

Marie laughed smokily, her breath quickening at what she read in his eyes.

'Blame it on the hot sun,' she said, and he nodded.

'Probably. Self-induced temporary madness, is that it?

Something behind that was disconcerting, made her think of the warning voices that had been playing intermittently in her head ever since she first became involved with him, but then the thought slid away, and she half closed her eyes, feeling warm and languorous.

It seemed absolutely right to feel his lips on hers, moving with slow, leisurely persuasion, his moist tongue unhurriedly exploring her mouth. She moaned, her eyes still closed, and wrapped her arms behind his head. He pulled her so that she was facing him, both of them on their sides, and parted her legs with his thigh.

The feel of his leg rubbing against her most intimate area made her moan again, more urgently.

She wondered what would happen if someone came strolling along, but the beach was quiet and deserted and anyway they were far back on the beach, relatively sheltered from casual eyes. She felt his fingers unhook the back of the strapless bikini, which immediately fell to one side, exposing the pale swell of her breast.

'Beautiful,' she heard him say under his breath, and he pushed her slightly so that she was lying flat on the towel, then he cupped her breast with his hand and caressed it until she wanted to thrash about with frustrated yearning.

His mouth trailed over her shoulders, nipping her skin, then down to her breasts, and he nuzzled against her nipple, teasing it with his tongue until she moaned huskily, her head flung back in abandon.

He slipped his hand under her bikini and the feel of his fingers against her was unbearable.

'We shouldn't,' she protested breathlessly, and he murmured, 'Why not?'

'What if someone comes along?'

'No one will come along. Besides, no one can see us from the beach.'

'I'm not sure,' she said uncertainly. 'I don't want you to think that I do this…'

'I don't,' he said gravely. 'If I did, I wouldn't be here now, believe me. But if you want to stop right here, then that's your prerogative.'

'It's just that I don't want…I couldn't bear it,' she sighed with some desperation.

He placed his finger over her lips. 'I can't analyse what we feel for each other,' he said, 'but whatever it is, it's powerful. Talking about the future will just spoil this magic.'

Yes it would, she thought. This was a special feeling that was meant to be enjoyed, not debated. She had fallen in love with him and why should she pick it to pieces instead of simply enjoying it? It would work out in the end, she was sure.

He slipped her bikini bottom off, and as he caressed her with the palm of his hand until she was moist and aching, she thought that she had gone past the point of no return anyway. Someone would have to approach them on a galloping horse accompanied by a barking dog if she were even to be aware of their presence.

There were no such noises as their lovemaking intensified. Only the calm background slap of the waves rippling up to the shoreline, then ebbing away, and the rustle of coconut trees in the breeze. The sound of her heart pounding in her chest was louder than the noises of nature around them.

He was gentle with her. He took his time, waiting for the right moment to complete their act of lovemaking. She had not told him that she was a virgin, but he must have made that assumption because she could remember telling him about her lack of boyfriends. He had also assumed that she was using some form of contraception, and she had not disillusioned him. Why should she? She was in her safe-as-houses period anyway.

'You're incredible,' he whispered later, softly, into her ear, and she smiled with her eyes closed. She felt incredible. She felt absolutely wonderful. She felt as though she had been shown for the first time her reason for living. She felt like a woman in love, and it was amazing. She had no idea how she was going to face everyone on the ship. They would all guess, they would all be able to see that she was different.

She smiled up at him, wondrously happy, surprised and thrilled that this man, this virtual stranger, had been able to reach inside her to the woman waiting to get out. She didn't want to think about the future, she knew that it was too soon, but she was certain that all those obstacles which her silent, reasoning mind had laboriously pointed out could be surmounted. They were wildly different from each other, as his mother had informed her in no uncertain terms, but hurdles were part and parcel of love.

She wound her arms around his neck, loving the glint of passion that flared in his eyes, and felt any doubts she might have had ebbing away like the tide from the shore.

CHAPTER THREE

MARIE found that she was tiptoeing. She worked on this ship, but right now she felt like an intruder, stealthily creeping along the carpeted corridor, which at eleven o'clock was deserted. Nearly everyone was in the Show Room, being entertained by a cabaret. She should know, she had just been there herself, serving drinks, smiling, chatting to the guests, and all the time itching to get away.

A whole day without Holden. It had felt like a century. By ten o'clock she had felt like an addict suffering keen withdrawal symptoms. She just wanted to be with him, to touch him. When she had seen him sitting with his mother at the back of the room, staring idly at the cabaret while his mother chatted away at him from her chair, she had decided on the spot that she would wait until he had left, then she would surprise him in his room.

It was an appalling breach of regulations and she had felt slightly horrified that she was prepared to go to such lengths for a few minutes' private chat, but what alternative did she have? He had spotted her in the Show Room, had followed her with his eyes, but she had been too busy even to think of venturing over to his table.

Apart from the fact that someone else was dealing with that part of the room, there was the small drawback of his mother. Mrs Greystone didn't like her. She had made that abundantly clear from the outset, and she had missed no opportunity to emphasise the fact every time she happened to see Marie. Why court antagonism by trying to engage her son in conversation when she could see him alone in his room later on?

Her eyes were flicking excitedly at the cabin doors. She had never been in this section of the ship before. This was the deck that housed the de luxe suites. Holden was staying in the Penthouse Suite. She had curiously asked him what it was like a few days previously, and he had listed off the various features, amused at her expression.

'It sounds like an apartment,' she had told him, sighing. 'Who on earth can afford to stay somewhere like that?'

He had shrugged. 'You'd be surprised. There's more wealth lying about than you imagine.'

'Is that why your mother is so concerned for your welfare?' Marie had asked, looking up at him and grinning. 'Does she want to make sure that no one unsuitable dips into your reserves?'

His expression had tightened. 'Protective, isn't she? Although I'd agree that the world is full of parasites.' His expression had been cold as he had said that, and it hadn't taken a wild stretch of imagination to figure out that he would have no compunction in dealing with those parasites.

She paused at the end and frowned. This was the suite and the door was slightly ajar. She looked around the deserted corridor, wondering whether she should push open the door and make sure that everything was all right inside. She hovered, inching forward, reaching out towards the door-knob, then she drew back.

She could hear voices. He was with his mother. She recognised that cultured voice immediately, and for the first time in her life she did something that she had never dreamed of doing before. She listened. Had it been her imagination or had she heard her name being mentioned?

She bit her lip nervously, torn between sneaking back the way she had come and remaining where she was and, as she perched on the edge of indecision, she heard his mother say, 'You're a fool. The girl is taking you for a ride. Really, Holden, can't you see it?' The voice was coming from the right, sharp, insistent, demanding a response, but there was none and she continued in the same quick, urgent tone, 'I saw the way she was watching you tonight. She made sure that she looked away when she thought that I was looking, but I'm not an utter fool!'

'You're over-reacting, Mother.' Holden's voice was a lazy, vaguely bored drawl, and Marie could picture the expression on his face as clearly as if he had been standing in front of her. Cool, his grey eyes hooded, his mouth drawn into a forbidding line.

'I am not over-reacting!' Mrs Greystone said with more heat than Marie could have imagined possible. 'The girl is a member of the crew, for heaven's sake!'

'What are you suggesting, Mother?' he asked.

Leave now, Marie told herself, but her feet refused to obey the command. They remained glued to the spot.

'You know what I'm suggesting, Holden.'

'Do I?' Holden asked coldly. 'Spell it out for me.'

'I will. This girl is not your type...'

'You have no idea what type of girl I find attractive!'

'She's a gold-digger,' Mrs Greystone continued implacably. 'She knows who you are, she knows you're worth a great deal of money. Of course she wants to capitalise on the situation.'

Holden laughed. 'Really, Mother, you don't have an awful lot of confidence in my sex appeal if you're implying that the only way I can attract a girl is through my wallet.'

'This is not funny, Holden! Remember your father!'

'I'd rather not,' Holden said sharply.

'Fine, but all I'm saying is that she's not the sort to be interested in a shipboard romance.'

'I haven't proposed to her, for God's sake.' He was beginning to sound impatient.

'Good, just so long as you keep it that way. I don't wish to interfere in your private life, but—'

'Mother—' his voice was closer now '—I have no intention of…' He was nearly at the door! Marie turned and fled. Her face was burning. She reached the end of the corridor just as Holden shut the cabin door, and she breathed a shuddering sigh of relief.

What had he been about to say? Her brain feverishly supplied the humiliating answer. I have no intention of marrying the girl. She's a fling!

She walked quickly back to her cabin, head down, her brain whirring with unpleasant thoughts. She shouldn't have remained there, she shouldn't have listened to that conversation, but then, she thought feverishly, wasn't the truth preferable to a fool's paradise?

Holden Greystone found her attractive, but he wasn't about to take her on as his life's commitment. She let herself into her small cabin, her fingers trembling as they fumbled with the key. She felt sick and humiliated.

Everything had been going so well. What they had was something special, at least to her, but, she thought bitterly, not to him. To him, she was a member of the crew. He thought along the same lines as his mother, even if he denied it. I have no intention of… She began undressing, tossing her clothes on the bed, and replaying that overheard conversation in her head until she felt as though her brain were going to explode.

She had been so trusting. Now she felt sick with misery that that trust had been taken and used. Holden Greystone was an experienced man and he had turned that experience on her. From the very first moment he had set eyes on her he had wanted her, and he really hadn't had to try awfully hard, had he? She had probably been one of his easier conquests. Or perhaps they were all easy. Maybe that accounted for his easy, self-assured charm, that air of command.

The more she thought about it, the more sickened she became. She felt consumed with self-contempt. She would have to break it off, she decided. She wasn't about to become his little fling until he became bored with her, and ready to take his talents elsewhere.

She flung herself on to the bed and buried her head under the pillow.

Life had not prepared her for this. Her mother had died before she could shed her wisdom of the ways of men, and her aunt had simply pursed her lips whenever the opposite sex was mentioned.

She had gone through life untouched and untempted. Easy prey for a man like Holden, she thought, bitterly resentful.

Her eyes were sore and heavy the following morning. It was early. Five-thirty. She looked outside and saw that it was already light. The sky was pale blue, but in a couple of hours' time it would be aquamarine and blazing hot. Frankly, she wished that it would rain. She felt that she could cope with rain, and for the first time she wished that she were back in England, back in her aunt's house and very far away from blue skies and blue seas and happy faces.

She dressed quickly, only dashing on some light make-up as an afterthought, and then took a deep breath.

She was going to smile, smile, smile if it killed her.

When she reached the kitchens, she found that she really didn't have to try too hard. Everyone was dashing around, getting ready for breakfast. The chef was scowling, muttering under his breath about chaos not being the right atmosphere for someone as creative as he was, a familiar lament to which he invariably received the familiar responses of wide, unsympathetic grins.

Marie threw herself into the fray, and the next time she emerged was when the last of the passengers had strolled out of the dining-room, full, fed and happy.

She hadn't expected to see Holden there. He had arranged to meet her in her cabin after breakfast, and she winced at her remembered pleasure at the rendezvous. It had been so easy to fall in love, she thought bitterly. Untouched, untempted, she had been ripe for the picking by a man like Holden, and in her heady, starry-eyed excitement, she had managed to persuade herself that their relationship could fight the odds, even though, in retrospect, he had said nothing along those lines. With the warmth of the sun they had both been swept out of time, and she had been fool enough not to see reality casting its shadow around the corner.

She waited for him anxiously, her stomach knotted with tension, but in fact when she did hear a knock on the door it was to discover that it was Jessica, wearing a concerned frown and a tea-and-sympathy expression.

She looked at Marie's face and then said, dispensing with the preliminaries, 'You looked odd this morning, so I thought I'd find out what's wrong.'

Marie gave her a watery smile. 'Nothing's wrong,' she said. 'Nothing incurable, anyway.'

'It's that man, isn't it?' she asked, and Marie nodded, not seeing the point in lying. 'I might have guessed. He smelled of danger the first time I laid eyes on him.

Something about the way he moved, the way he spoke.'
She looked sympathetic. 'I should have said something, I
suppose. We're the same age, I know, but you make me
feel like a hundred.'

'Oh, no, I should have used my brain,' Marie muttered
bitterly. 'Fortunately, it's in gear now.'

'Who *is* he anyway?' Jessica didn't wait for the question to be answered. She looked thoughtful and continued,
'We've speculated a bit, and come to the conclusion that
he's someone Very Important, which is why there hasn't
been a whisper of discontent over what's been going on.'

'Very Important,' Marie said dully.

'Cheer up. Very Important often spells Big Trouble,
and I should know. I made a similar mistake a few months
ago, hence my relief at being here on the high seas.' She
smiled with regret. 'My Very Important man happened to
be my boss, and he also happened to be married. God
knows how I could have fallen for the wife-doesn't-
understand-me routine, but I did, and it was a mess.' She
smiled and squeezed Marie's hand. 'Face it, the sea is full
of other fish.'

'You're right.'

'Some of the fish are very rich,' Jessica said in a deep,
conspiratorial voice. 'This liner alone testifies to my the-
ory.'

Marie laughed, but it sounded hollow. 'You've been
checking the passenger lists?' she asked with mock horror.

'Routine scanning,' Jessica answered, relief on her face
that she had at least persuaded Marie into talking. 'I sug-
gest you look around for another suitable match.'

Marie felt her heart constrict, but she smiled wanly.
'Any suggestions?'

'I'll keep my eyes open. I—'

'Will you indeed?' His voice was as cold as the eyes

that looked her over from the door, which had been wide open.

Jessica went bright red and looked like a goldfish being starved of water, then she shot out of the door, head bent, eyes down, back stiff.

Marie looked at him with defiance. So what if he had overheard the tail end of a seemingly incriminating conversation? They were evens now then, weren't they?

He stepped into the room and closed the door behind him, then he stared at her, his eyes icy.

'I didn't realise that I would have been interrupting such an illuminating little chat,' he said, in a voice which sent a chill snaking along her spine.

Polite, she thought bitterly, keep it polite, and for God's sake try not to let that naked masculinity play havoc with your brain. She met his stare without flinching.

'You shouldn't listen at doors, then,' she said, folding her arms.

'But one can discover so much that way sometimes,' he said, moving towards her, and she nodded, bitterly.

'Yes. How true.'

She felt a surge of fear and apprehension. So far she had only ever seen the warm, sensual, charming side of him, the side which he had, she thought acidly, aired because he considered that the fastest route to bed.

The ruthless cruelty she had felt, rather than experienced. Now the grey chill in his eyes reminded her that it was there, as much a part of him as the dry humour and the sexy smile. As much a part of him as the exploiting opportunist who had crooked his finger at her and never for a minute doubted that she would come running.

'A little careless to discuss gold-digging opportunities with the door open, wasn't it?' he asked, standing right in front of her, every lean, muscled line of his body a threat. His voice was low, controlled and deadly.

She had rehearsed what she was going to say to him, how she was going to break it off, but now that he was here and jumping to all the wrong conclusions, she realised that she didn't have to say much after all. She simply had to leave him with the mistaken impression that she had been after his money. He would find that easy enough to believe. Suspicion was second nature to a man like him.

'Answer me when I'm talking to you!' he roared, when she didn't say anything.

'Ssh,' Marie hissed desperately. 'Someone will hear you!'

'I have no intention of keeping my voice down! I own this bloody ship!'

His hands were in his pockets, but they were balled into tight fists. She could see the outline of them through the khaki material. Did he want to hit her? He looked it, that was certain. He looked as though he wanted to throttle her, but he wouldn't. He was not a man to indulge in physical violence. In fact he abhorred it. He had told her so himself. She had no reason to be scared but she was. Terrified. Terrified of that derisive, angry glint in his eyes which were cold and flat, like icy seas on a winter's day.

'What do you want me to say?' she asked, sticking her chin out and blinking hard. 'Do you want me to tell you that I was only after your money? All right, then, I was only after your money. Satisfied?'

He looked as if he would explode. He strode to the door and slammed it shut, then turned back to face her.

'So how long have you been plotting behind my back?' he asked. 'You must have thought you had found the goose that lays the golden eggs when I showed an interest in you.'

'Believe what you want,' she said, looking down, and he cupped her face in his hands, forcing her to look at him.

'When did you decide to take me for a ride?' he asked, and her eyes flared angrily.

'I don't suppose you would believe me if I told you that your money didn't mean a thing to me, would you?'

'After what I just heard?'

'Jessica was having a laugh!'

'You must think I'm a complete fool, darling,' he grated. 'It's too late for you. You can't wriggle out of it now. I just want you to tell me when you concocted your little plan, because I want to make damn sure that I never get taken in by someone like you in my life again.'

That hurt, but she didn't show it. I don't care, she told herself viciously. How can I care about someone whose only intention was to use me and then toss me aside like an old shoe that's outgrown its master's taste? She felt the painful bitterness rise up again in her throat.

He took a step towards her and she instinctively pressed back, although there was nowhere for her to go.

'Go away and leave me alone,' she whispered.

'Not yet, sweetheart. No one takes me for a fool.'

'I wish you had never come into my life,' she said with feeling. 'You should stick to the women you know, the women your mother approves of! Then you wouldn't be unfortunate enough to run into people like me, would you? Nobodies from nowhere who are a threat to that wonderful fortune of yours!'

His face was hard and savage but, worse than that, he was looking at her as if seeing her for the first time.

The accumulated anger and hurt and disillusionment swept through her in a rush, and words came spilling out.

'You go on and on about women being after you for

your money, but you never stop to think that you don't
do too badly when it comes to exploiting them, do you?
Face it, women are toys for you. You go through life
picking them up and discarding them without a backward
glance! Money has given you the right to act as though
feelings are worth nothing! If you want to think that I was
after your money, then go ahead, but if that thought had
never crossed your mind, tell me how long you would
have continued this relationship! Until I had stopped
amusing you? Until my gaucheness had ceased to be a
little novelty? And then what would you have done?
Moved on! Now don't you think that that's exploitation
of a worse sort?'

His eyes narrowed to slits. 'Poor little Marie Stephens,'
he said with a humourless smile, 'had you hoped for
something bigger? Marriage, perhaps? Was it a shock to
you when I didn't feed you a few fairy-stories about the
happy-ever-after life?'

'No!' she denied, but colour had flooded into her face.
Had she really expected marriage out of this relationship?
Maybe, she realised now, she hadn't, not to start with. To
start with, she had been content to go with the flow, to
be at the mercy of her newly awakened emotions, to bask
in that wild excitement of knowing that she was the object
of his passion. A lot of women, she had known instinctively, would have found that wildly exciting. Holden
Greystone was not a man to be ignored. His tall, lean
masculinity demanded attention, and that lazy, persuasive
charm could woo the birds from the trees.

But very soon she had begun to nurture silent dreams.
The magic of what was happening to her had blinded her
and she was paying for her insanity.

'I wouldn't marry you if you were the last person on
earth!' she threw at him. 'It's so easy to believe that you

can't fail to be the object of attraction to the whole of the female sex, but I don't suppose it's even crossed your mind that I might just not be interested in getting involved with you?'

'Are you saying that if I had proposed to you you would have turned me down flat? That a grubby little gold-digger would have been satisfied with a few trinkets and baubles?' He laughed, and it was a cruel, grating sound.

'I never wanted your money,' she said with deep resentment, 'and you're the last man I'd ever choose to marry. I enjoyed the time we spent together, and you did me a favour in a way, because before you came along I was nothing more than a naïve child, but I was going to finish what we had anyway. I was going to tell you that it was time we called it a day.'

'I did you a favour?' he asked with cold, scathing disdain. 'I did *you* a favour?'

Marie kept her eyes fixed on the wall behind him. She could see the sky through the tiny window. It was clear and blue. Things like this, soul-shattering confrontations like these, should never happen on hot, cloudless days. This was the kind of day to be enjoyed, and right now she couldn't remember having ever felt so miserable in her life before. At fourteen, she had imagined that she could never hurt again, that her quota of pain had been exhausted when her parents had died. Now, seven years later, she knew that there were different kinds of pain, but they all hurt.

'You were bored,' she flung at him recklessly, no longer caring what she said because from where she was standing things couldn't get much worse than this, 'and whether I was after your money or not, you might just stop to think that I was bored as well!'

'Is that a fact?' he said with icy calm. 'But since you're saying that we used each other, why stop now?' He pulled her towards him. His hands tightened into her hair, hurting her. He wanted to hurt her, she realised. His lips, as they bore down on hers, were hard and merciless. His mouth moved against hers, but there was no tenderness in it. It was hard to think that this was the same man who had made her laugh, whose lovemaking had made her moan in ecstasy. She struggled against him, but that only intensified the savagery of his lips. His hand in the small of her back forced her against him and she realised, with horror, that her body was responding to his naked animal attraction. Her legs were unsteady and she could feel a heady moistness rushing through her.

She held herself rigid, and finally he drew back, his grey eyes as hard as flint.

'I must have been mad ever to have got involved with you.' He had hurt her and she really wanted to hurt him back, she wanted him to feel something of the pain she was feeling at having her whole life knocked into ruins. 'I would never have become involved with you if it weren't for Jessica!'

'What are you saying?' he asked, in a dangerously calm voice. He had drawn back from her and she didn't dare meet his eyes. She hated herself, she just wanted to crawl away into some hole somewhere and wait for this phase in her life to blow over. He wanted a gold-digger, though, she thought with burning bitterness, then why not give him one?

'We made a bet,' she heard herself say. 'Yes, we made a bet that I could…'

There was a deathly silence. She wished that she could retract the words. She had been under attack and she had reacted on impulse. Dangerous impulse.

'I see. The truth comes out.'

'Look,' she said, 'I shouldn't have—'

'Please,' he interrupted in a smooth, calm voice, 'don't launch into any explanations. I get the picture in all its sordid detail. How did you decide which one of you got the walk-on part? Did you toss a coin? Heads your friend, tails you? I saw you first, but did you think that your friend might just as easily have enticed me into a relationship if she won the bet?'

'No...'

'And did you find me a challenge, sweetheart? Did I live up to your expectations? You make me sick.'

Marie stared at him, not knowing what to say. She knew that she shouldn't really care what he said because after today he would no longer even feature in her life, but she found that she did care. He had accused her of being a gold-digger, and she didn't want to see that scathing disdain in his eyes, but, she told herself fiercely, all's fair in love and war, isn't it? He wanted me as his part-time lover, and for all his talk about my being after his money, he wouldn't have shown an ounce of compunction when it came to throwing me over. Would he?

He was looking at her fixedly, as if she were something that had crawled out from under a rock. Eventually he said politely, 'I don't think there's a great deal left to be said, do you?'

'No.' She struggled to speak through stiff lips.

'In that case, if you don't mind getting out of my way, I'll be going.'

'Of course.' She stepped aside and he brushed past her to the door. On impulse, she said in a small, flat voice, 'Will you be staying on?'

'Oh, I don't think so.' His eyes met hers and she unwillingly held his stare, even though the blood had rushed to her head, making her giddy. 'I should get you and your friend thrown off this ship,' he told her, 'but quite frankly, when I leave this room, I don't want your name ever to pass my lips again.' His lips twisted into a cruel sneer. 'So you'll be relieved to know that you'll be free to indulge in your little games to your heart's content.'

She couldn't believe that she would never see him again. When she had overheard that conversation, pride had rushed in, rallying her forces together, insisting that the only option was to break things off. She hadn't expected things to develop the way that they had. He had misconstrued everything and it didn't matter that the net result was the same. They were finished.

It was for the best. She had not wanted to get hurt. She had been through enough hurt in her life. When her parents had died, it had left a gaping hole in her life. She had been rudderless, lonely and afraid. All this time later, the hurt had subsided, lost its teeth, but it was still there like the melancholy refrain of a song that was impossible to forget.

She had always wanted the thrill of love, the excitement of romance, a wonderful adventure, and Fate had cruelly given her all those things, but what it had given with one hand it had taken with the other. Holden Greystone had made every man she had ever met seem like a grey shadow, and her own stupidity had put her common sense on hold. She had tasted the sweetness of love, but not without experiencing the bitterness of regret, and it made no difference trying to console herself with the thought that this was all a damage-limiting exercise in the long run. That survival made sure that you forgot and carried on.

He gave her one last derisive glance, and then he was gone.

Marie slumped back into the room, pulling down the bed and sitting on it.

Funny, but her mind seemed to be completely blank, like someone who had had a severe shock. It reminded her horribly of how she had felt when she had learned of her parents' death, as though she had been turned to stone.

Ten minutes ago her head had been throbbing from the million and one thoughts battering away at her. She lay down on the bed and stared sightlessly at the ceiling. Now she couldn't even muster up a coherent line of thought.

She had no idea how much time passed. Someone knocked on the door, and she held her breath, waiting for them to go away, and eventually they did.

She kept telling herself the same thing over and over again: it hurts now, but in six months' time it will have faded. Pain like this couldn't last forever.

She would never see Holden Greystone again, and that was the way it should be.

CHAPTER FOUR

GREYSTONE Inc. was a huge building in the financial district in London. It rose up into the sky like an enormous black glass monster. Marie stood outside in her apricot cotton dress and stared up at it with a sinking heart.

It had been difficult enough making this trip, but she might have felt a little braver if she had been confronted with something less grand, less overpowering. She felt an uneasy stirring in the pit of her stomach. Holden Greystone was like this building, she thought, hard, overpowering, menacing, and there was no point in trying to kid herself otherwise. There was no point in indulging in the pleasant fantasy that time might have changed him, mellowed him. She was here now, and she had to be realistic.

The building was approached by shallow steps. She walked up these very slowly, head bent, hands in the pockets of her dress, and her bag slung over one shoulder.

She had thought long and hard about what she should wear this morning. She did not possess a business suit, which would have been her first option, and she didn't have the money to spare to buy one, so she had settled for the next best thing. The apricot dress was straight, with small buttons down the front. No frills, no flounces, nothing that might mentally put her at a disadvantage when she finally met him face to face. Her shoes were flat and sensible, her bag was small and sensible and the short bob

framing her face was neatly brushed and, she hoped, like-
wise sensible. Sensible, practical and in control was how
she wanted to appear.

'Practical and a little daunting,' had been her aunt's
verdict, 'like a schoolteacher.'

'Good,' Marie had said, frowning back into the mirror
in the hallway. 'Wish me luck.'

'You won't need it,' her aunt had smiled. 'You'll be
fine.'

Marie thought back to this conversation now. If someone had told her, when she was fourteen and an unwilling
lodger in that little house in North London, that her aunt
would one day prove to be her greatest ally, she would
have shaken her head in disbelief. Those fine, pursed lips,
she had thought, could never smile, those unforgiving
eyes could never show warmth, but she was to be proved
wrong. People changed, didn't they? She had changed,
after all. She had grown up, but then experiences were
great at catapulting you into adulthood. She could hardly
remember what it had been like in those few heady weeks
when she had been bowled over by Holden Greystone. It
was incredible to think that she had ever been that naïve
and trusting.

But then again, three years is a long time, she thought.

She slipped through the revolving glass door and found
herself in a large, airy reception lounge. There were plants
everywhere, and two trees flanked the circular reception
desk in the middle of the atrium. There were lifts towards
the back, and at the front several low chairs and sofas,
and coffee-tables with stacks of business magazines taste-
fully arranged on them.

Marie glanced around her and took a deep breath. None
of this was making her feel any easier. Of course, he
might be in a meeting, or out of the country, or anything

for that matter. She had not telephoned to make an appointment because she wanted to rely on the one advantage she had which was the element of surprise. She didn't want to allow him any time to mull things over. And, she admitted honestly to herself, she didn't want to speak to him on the telephone. If she had to confront him, then she preferred to go the whole hog and confront him face to face.

She tried to remember all the reassuring things that her aunt had had to say on the matter, but she could only come up with the same thought. She needed him and that was that. Like it or not, face him she must.

The receptionist was a young girl with bright brown eyes and shoulder-length brown hair which was tucked behind her ears.

Hurdle number one, Marie thought, approaching the desk. She smiled and asked whether Mr Greystone, Mr Holden Greystone, was available.

It was the first time she had spoken his name aloud to anyone, apart from her aunt. The first time in three long years. His image, which she had fooled herself into imagining had receded to the back of her mind in some convenient storage area labelled 'The Past', sprang up at her with such graphic clarity that her mouth went dry. Tall, vibrant, sexy, his grey eyes as changing as the sea, alluring one minute, frightening the next. She remembered the last time she had seen him, in that small cabin on the ship. His eyes had been cold and hostile then, glinting at her with dislike. Even now, she could remember every word that had been spoken between them and she had to make an effort to clear her head of the unpleasant memories. It was no use delving back into the past, she thought. What purpose would that serve? It would only make her more apprehensive than she already felt.

The receptionist was smiling at her, her brown eyes curious, but she didn't ask any questions. She leafed down the book on the desk in front of her and nodded.

'He's in all day,' she said, 'but I'm afraid I don't know what meetings he has lined up. Have you an appointment?'

Marie shook her head. 'I'm afraid not. I found myself in this part of the world today and I thought I might look him up. I'm—' she paused '—an old acquaintance.' She had almost said 'old friend', but that would have been a staggering exaggeration. Even acquaintance, as a description, left a lot to be desired.

It crossed her mind that he might not even remember her, although he had struck her as a man who never forgot.

The receptionist looked at her hesitantly, and Marie said quickly, because she had to see him, she could not possibly leave this building without doing so, 'I haven't spoken to him for three years, and I really would like to see him, if I may.'

'Three years? Have you been out of the country? I'm sorry, it's none of my business.'

'Out of the country? No,' Marie replied slowly, 'not out of the country. Just…busy. Time ran away and when I next looked at the calendar I was three years older!' She hoped that the young girl wouldn't see the urgency on her face.

'His office is on the tenth floor,' she said, scrutinising her with friendly, lively curiosity now. 'I'm sure Mrs Haven wouldn't mind if you went up.'

'Mrs Haven?'

'His personal assistant. She'll be able to tell you when he's around.'

Marie smiled with a mixture of relief that this hurdle had been surmounted, and terror at what that meant.

There was no one in the lift as she pressed the button and the doors closed with a soft swish. She closed her eyes and made an effort not to succumb to the mounting panic inside her.

When the doors next opened she found herself staring down a corridor which was carpeted in a thick, pale blue carpet, and which was flanked on either side by several doors and glass partitions. This was the directors' floor, she assumed. The outer offices were clearly where the personal assistants worked, and beyond them, through connecting doors, were their bosses' offices.

Marie walked along the corridor, her eyes flicking to the nameplates outside the offices, occasionally receiving curious glances from some of the secretaries behind their word processors. There was no hustle and bustle in here. Everything was hushed and a little intimidating.

Holden's office was the one at the very end. Marie looked at the gold nameplate outside with a gut-wrenching sense of inevitability.

'Don't be afraid,' her aunt had said, 'he's only human. He can't eat you.'

That being the case, why then did she feel as though she were about to walk into a lion's den?

Mrs Haven looked up from what she was doing as Marie entered the office. She was a middle-aged woman, plump, with dark hair flecked with strands of grey. There was a pile of work on the desk next to her computer terminal, as well as two telephones and a small fax machine. Against the wall was a photocopier which was switched on and hummed very softly into the silence. It was an efficient-looking room. No pictures apart from a print of the cruise liner, which brought a hard knot into

Marie's chest, and a calendar. There were quite a few plants, however, one large one in the corner of the room, several small ones against the wall on a shelf which also housed what appeared to be law manuals and financial directories.

'Have you an appointment, Miss...?'

Marie approached the desk warily, her eyes flicking to the mahogany door behind her. Was Holden Greystone behind that door? she wondered.

'I'm afraid not.' She smiled and tried to look natural. If the other woman detected even the slightest hint of apprehension behind that smile, she would probably have the security guards running up here in no time at all. She trotted off the same story she had told the brown-haired receptionist, in an apologetic voice.

'Mr Greystone is in,' the older woman said, looking at her sharply. 'He's due out in a few minutes, though. He has a meeting in the boardroom. Perhaps he'll see you, if I could have your name?'

'Can I surprise him?' She smiled a natural, warm smile, while her insides did a rumba that threatened to bring up everything she had had for breakfast.

It worked, though. She found herself standing at that mahogany door and, with her back to his secretary, she squeezed her eyes tightly shut and then opened them again, before knocking briskly, confidently, on the door, like the old friend that she most definitely was not.

'Yes!'

The same voice. The same dark, deep voice that had haunted her dreams for months after she had left the cruise liner and returned to London. Well, she thought, trying to manufacture some self-confidence, his voice isn't going to change, is it?

She pushed open the door and wished that need had not driven her here to this place, to see this man.

He was on the telephone, and he didn't even look up when she entered. He thought that it was Mrs Haven, she realised. It gave her a few precious seconds to observe him, to see how much he hadn't changed.

In all the time she had known him, she had never seen him formally dressed. He was wearing a white shirt with thin red stripes running down it and his tie, a plain dark grey one, was slung over one shoulder. The sleeves of his shirt were rolled to the elbows, exposing his forearms, with their sprinkling of dark hair.

Memory and reality fused into one, and for a second she felt a blinding desire to rush out of the room; then she remembered why she was here, why she had to be here.

When he looked up at her, it was like being at the receiving end of a massive electric shock. She hadn't really expected Holden Greystone to have changed, had she? Three years had not altered his features. It was the same hard, arrogant face staring at her now, the grey eyes expressing surprise, or maybe shock, she couldn't be sure.

He had been in the middle of a sentence. He said something abrupt down the line and replaced the receiver, then he sat back in his leather chair with his fingers linked and stared at her. The shock had left his face but there was no pleasure there now as he surveyed her.

Marie looked back at him wordlessly.

'Well, well, well,' he said at last, 'and look at what the cat brought in. What are you doing here? How did you get past my secretary?' The questions were fired at her like bullets.

She didn't dare move. Her feet were locked to the ground.

'Well? Answer me!'

'I said that I was an old friend.' Marie found her voice and there was high-pitched defiance in it. 'I said that I happened to be in the area.'

Now that he was looking directly at her she could see that he had changed. There was an austerity about him now; he looked tough, unforgiving, the perfectly sculpted face darker and more angular than she had remembered.

'Sit down!'

She moved towards the chair opposite him and sat. She couldn't take her eyes off him. She was noticing every little detail about him, matching up the man in front of her to the memory she had carried about with her for three long years. There was a knock on the door and Mrs Haven entered, her eyes flicking between the two of them.

'Your appointment with Mr Pendle from the construction firm,' she said. 'He's arrived and he's waiting for you in the boardroom. Shall I tell him that you'll be along in a minute?'

'Cancel it.'

'But...surely...'

'You heard me. Cancel it!'

Mrs Haven exited in muddled confusion, and his attention returned to Marie. She moistened her lips. She would have to lead up gently, gradually to what she had to say, she decided. If he was hostile now, then God help her when he found out the reason for her visit. He would hit the proverbial roof. She smiled and said pleasantly, 'You haven't changed. How are you?'

'What have you come here for?'

He stood up, as if he could no longer bear the confines of the chair, and moved towards the window, staring out, his hands in his pockets, his sharp, perfect profile to her.

'I asked you a question!' he bit out, turning to face her,

perching against the window ledge, which, she was faintly amused to see, displayed a few pot plants, clearly Mrs Haven's idea since Holden Greystone looked like the last person in the world to indulge a taste for indoor gardening.

'You're making me nervous!' she returned hotly. 'Standing there, looking at me as if I'm a criminal!'

'How would you like me to look at you?'

'You could try with a bit of common politeness.'

'I don't recall having invited you into my office. I don't recall having decided to get in touch with you after three years. Why the hell should I talk to you with a bit of common politeness?' His voice was a snarl, and he moved towards her to sit on the edge of his desk, his arms folded.

'Did you come here as a *bet*?' he asked contemptuously. 'Did you and your friend decide to have another giggle at my expense? If so, then I'm warning you, it'll be a mistake you'll live to regret.'

She had forgotten how frightening he could be. She could feel herself cringing back in the chair.

'Don't you threaten me!' she said. 'I'm not here as a…a bet.' She lowered her eyes, and when she next looked at him she tried another attempt at a smile. She had to get him into a more reasonable mood, she thought. 'Look,' she said evenly, 'it's been three years, and I know we parted company…on slightly unfriendly terms, but can't we try to put that behind us?'

The telephone rang from behind him and he snatched it up, watching her as he spoke into it, his voice impatient and restless. He hated her, she realised. She had, in his eyes, insulted his sense of judgement three years ago and he had never forgiven her. It was pointless trying to cajole him into being reasonable. As far as he was concerned she was a regrettable incident that belonged to the past.

When he replaced the receiver, it was with a gentle click. He no longer looked furiously at her, as if she were something profoundly distasteful that had suddenly reappeared when he had assumed that it had been safely disposed of. He wasn't smiling, though. His expression was one of icy mockery.

'So you want us to be adult, Marie.' He stood up and gazed down at her with a mirthless smile. 'Why not? After all, you're right, we are old friends. Or maybe not quite friends, but then we did sleep together, didn't we? So that must qualify us for some category, don't you think?' He strolled around his desk to fetch his jacket from where it was resting on the back of the leather swivel chair, and slung it casually over one shoulder, taking his time, every movement leisurely.

'Come on,' he said to her, and she looked at him bewildered.

'Come on where?'

'There's a wine bar just around the corner. Nice place. We can have lunch, a drink.' His lips twisted into another of those humourless smiles. 'An office is no place for past lovers to catch up, is it?'

Marie stood up reluctantly. Actually, the office was precisely where she should have liked to remain. She was here for a purpose, and she didn't want to lose sight of that purpose in the informal, intimate ambience of a wine bar. It was bad enough facing him across a desk. It would be ten times worse facing him across a cup of coffee with music playing in the background.

He wasn't about to argue about it, though. He was already at the door, waiting for her.

He was leaner than she remembered. Had he lost weight? Maybe it was seeing him in a suit, formally dressed. Maybe that made him look so predatory and dangerous.

He opened the door and she brushed past him, her arm tingling uncomfortably from where it had come into contact with him. Mrs Haven looked up as they came out, her plump face showing worried bewilderment.

'When will you be back, Mr Greystone?' she asked.

He said with a shrug, 'Later. You'll have to cancel all my appointments for today.' His eyes slid to where Marie was standing by the outer door. 'I have a lot of catching up to do with my old friend here. Fend off my calls, would you? I've got some letters to be typed on my desk—make sure that you get that one off to Jeffries, it's important.'

Mrs Haven was looking at him, in the most respectful manner possible, as though he had gone completely mad, but she nodded when he finished talking, watching them as they left the office.

'There's no need to miss anything on my behalf,' Marie said, turning to him as they waited for the lift to arrive.

'Oh, I think I shall have to, don't you?' His grey eyes skimmed over her with lazy appraisal. 'You're here for a reason, and whatever that reason is, you want to take your time about it. Am I right?' When she didn't answer, he said coolly, 'I admit, I was shocked to see you when you first arrived, but I'm quite prepared to go along and play our adult game of exchanging social banter until you decide to tell me the reason for your little visit. Although I have to tell you that I can already guess what it is.'

'You can?' Her heart skipped a beat and she told herself that he couldn't possibly even begin to guess her reason for this sudden visit. He would know soon enough, of course, and in fact she could tell him right now, but the thought of having to face that icy wrath so soon again made her shiver. The time isn't quite right, she told herself guiltily. I need a bit longer to build up my reserves of self-confidence, though she had to admit to herself that that was a bit optimistic.

He didn't reply. The lift had arrived, and he ushered her in, and for a while there was no opportunity to resume the conversation because it stopped at nearly every floor. She noticed, wryly, that everyone who entered greeted him with a certain amount of subservient awe, and looked at her with sidelong, curious glances. As soon as they step out of here, she thought, they'll all be asking each other the same questions. Who the hell is that woman? What's she doing with him? For the past two years she had worked in a small office and she knew enough about what went on in one to see that it was a hotbed of gossip, particularly where the big chiefs were concerned, and Holden Greystone was the biggest chief of them all.

He glanced at her with a wry look, and she knew instantly that he was aware of what was going on in her head, and that alarmed her. She almost preferred his hostility to that sudden, telepathic understanding that elicited unwanted intimacy.

The lift stopped at the ground floor, disgorging its cargo, and she began speaking hurriedly, trying to regain some of her composure, asking him about the company, while she walked alongside him, making sure to keep a safe distance. Keeping the tiger at bay. The thought shot through her head and she glanced at him from under her lashes. Tiger. It was an apt description, wasn't it? Powerful, lethal, beautiful.

They stepped out into the sun and began walking along the crowded pavements towards the wine bar. It was nearly lunchtime and packed. Very few tourists here, just hordes of smartly dressed women and men wearing the regulation dark business suits. That didn't, surprisingly,

make Holden blend in any the more, though. He still stood
out, commanding attention. She saw the way women's
eyes flicked across to him, appraising his maleness. It suddenly crossed her mind that he might be married. He
wasn't wearing a wedding-ring but that didn't mean a
great deal. Lots of married men didn't.

He didn't strike her as being married, though, or, if he
was, then marriage had not tamed him in the slightest.

'Here we are,' he said, breaking her train of thought
and she looked up to see that they were standing outside
one of those quaint, old-fashioned wine bars that went to
great lengths to be Typically English. Probably as expensive as hell. If this were in the heart of Oxford Street there
would have been a mile-long queue of tourists waiting to
get in, but although it was busy, it wasn't over-crowded
and they managed to get a corner table without much
trouble at all.

She glanced at the menu card and saw that there was a
reason why that had been possible. The prices were steep
and that probably meant that the average office worker
would have had to think twice about coming here for a
light lunch and a drink. An average office worker, she
thought with a certain amount of sadness, like myself. A
nine-to-fiver without the sort of money that could stretch
to the little luxuries in life like smoked salmon sandwiches or prawn and avocado baguettes.

'What would you like to drink?' he asked, waiting until
she was seated. 'Coffee or a glass of wine? If I remember
correctly, alcohol never held much temptation for you, no
even those exotic cocktails you could get in the West
Indies. But maybe you've changed?'

She might have guessed that there would have been a
sting behind even the most polite of questions, she
thought.

'A glass of mineral water, please,' she said, not rising to the bait, and he summoned a waiter across to take the order.

'Have something to eat,' he said in a voice which was more of an order than a request, and she obligingly glanced again at the menu.

She would have a prawn and salad sandwich, she told him, although, she thought, at the moment her stomach didn't feel up to much. It was running on nervous tension. There probably wouldn't be room even for something as innocuous as a sandwich.

'So...' He turned to her and shot her a laconic smile.

'So,' she returned, in a high, over-bright voice, 'how are you? Doing well, I see?'

'Is there a time limit for the chit-chat before you get down to business, Marie?' He gave her a long, cool look. 'If there is, then I could save us both some time by giving you a quick précis of the last three years of my life, and save you the bother of asking your polite little questions.'

He was drinking wine. He took a sip from his glass and continued to watch her.

'If you didn't want to come here, if you didn't want to see me, then all you had to do was to tell me to go away.' There were angry red patches on her cheeks. She didn't want to get angry. She couldn't afford to, but she couldn't seem to help herself.

'Oh, but you wouldn't have gone, would you?' He gave her a smile that fell only slightly short of being downright unpleasant.

'Why are you acting as though what happened between us happened yesterday instead of years ago? I would have—'

'Because,' he bit out, leaning forward, his face close to hers so that she could see every line, every pore, could breathe in his male scent, 'I haven't forgotten. It might just as well have been yesterday!'

Marie fell back, her heart thudding heavily.

'You can't mean that!'

'I damn well do! You took me for a ride.' There was hatred in those eyes and in the curling of his lips. 'You played me for a fool, and I haven't forgotten. Not one iota of it! I have never in my life been taken in by a pretty face and, like all mistakes, they prey on your mind until you feel as though you're going mad. When I left that cabin, I could have killed you. Now, for whatever reason you've come back, I can't say the feeling's changed that much. You still look like an angel, but now I know better!'

His attack startled her. Of course she had not expected him to welcome her with open arms, but this...!

'Then why are you here?' she asked in a low voice. 'Why didn't you just throw me out of your office?'

'Because I know what you're here for, and I wanted the satisfaction of hearing you beg for it.'

Every word was an attack and it left her shaken. The waiter approached them with their sandwiches and she breathed a sigh of relief that she could focus her attention on something else. Holden didn't even glance up. He continued to watch her broodingly from under his lashes, his mouth drawn in a tight, cold line. Three years ago she had played with fire, and the fire was waiting to consume her.

'Don't you like what I'm saying, Marie?' His mouth curved into a sneer. 'Then why don't you get up and walk out? The door's just over there. I'm not holding you prisoner.'

For a second, she very nearly did.

'I can't believe you've harboured this hatred for me all

this time,' she whispered uneasily, and he brought his fist down on the table, hard. Out of the corner of her eye she could see the people at the table nearest to theirs glance across surreptitiously. Waiting for something more dramatic to happen, she thought cynically.

'Can't you?' he ground out viciously.

'Life goes on.'

'Spare me your platitudes,' he muttered, taking another long sip of wine. He called the waiter across and ordered a scotch. He looked at her in silence until the drink was brought and nervously deposited on the table. No cheery chit-chat from this waiter, she noticed. He had the uncomfortable look of someone bringing a drink for a vicious dog with a reputation for biting.

He raised the glass to his lips and swallowed half the contents in one go.

'So,' he said, sitting back, 'tell me why you're here. Let me hear you say it.'

'Why don't you tell me?' she threw back at him, 'since you claim to know the reason.'

'Money,' he said coldly. 'What other reason? Don't tell me that you've discovered a sudden interest in my welfare, and don't tell me that you were just passing by, which is the fairy-story you spun to get yourself into my office in the first place.'

Her eyes widened in surprise and he took her surprise for agreement with his accusation.

'So I'm right, aren't I? You've run up some debts for yourself and you suddenly remembered the very rich Holden Greystone that you once knew. The golden opportunity that you were once forced to forefeit because you were stupid enough to have been discussing your money-grabbing plans with your friend, with the door wide open.' He finished his drink and she wondered uneasily whether he would summon the waiter across for another, but he didn't. He bit into his sandwich instead and she realised that she hadn't eaten a mouthful of hers. She had forgotten about it completely, in fact.

'And what lengths were you prepared to go to to get your hands on a bit of my money, my little darling? Shouldn't you have worn something more appropriate to the occasion? Or perhaps you thought that anything more obviously tantalising would have been a little lacking in subtlety?'

She continued to stare at him speechlessly and he smiled again, a cold, calculating smile.

'Still,' he said, 'there's something quite sexy in that neat little dress, but of course, I'd want some proof of intent before I commit myself to anything.'

The table separating them was narrow, a tiny little thing that allowed the wine bar to maximise on space. Before she could protest, he had reached across, his elbow on the surface, and his long fingers tangled into her hair. He pulled her towards him and their mouths met, hers opening with surprise and panic. She felt his tongue invade and, for a moment, she was whipped back in time. No one had touched her for a long time and she closed her eyes, yielding momentarily to the knife-sharp pleasure shooting through her.

Passion was a monster. It would devour you if you let it, and it was a very long time since she had felt passion. She had no defence against it, nor against the stirrings of her body as it responded to his touch.

His hand moved down the nape of her neck and her skin burnt where he touched it.

When he drew back from her, her eyes were dazed and she felt as if she had been caught up in a sudden whirlwind, only to be hurled back to ground with dizzying speed.

His grey eyes were icy. 'That'll do for starters,' he said, although his eyes were not nearly as detached as his voice was. 'And what are your terms and conditions? How much do you want? I shall have to know what you want the money for, of course.'

Marie found her voice at last.

'How dare you!'

'How dare I?' He laughed at that, but there was no amusement in his eyes. 'A bit late for the insulted approach, isn't it? What's the point anyway? We've established what you're here for, so why continue playing games?'

'We,' she said shakily, 'have established nothing of the sort! You may have thought that you had it all figured out, but you can't be right all the time, Holden!'

Her face was white and she had a dreadful feeling that she was only hanging on to the remnants of her self-control by a thread. This was something she had never expected. She had felt hot desire under that angry, cruel kiss, and she realised that as far as he was concerned, she was unfinished business. He hadn't got over her, as she had assumed that he would have. There might well have been a string of women after her, but she was still the one who had proved him, at least in his eyes, a fool.

'I'm not here for your money,' she said, speaking quietly. The sandwich was still untouched on her plate. She could see the nervous waiter hovering in the distance, eyeing their plates, wondering whether he dared take the plunge and whip them away. Tables had to be cleared, after all.

He looked at her with mocking disbelief. 'No? Then do explain why you're here. I'm on the edge of my seat.

You'll have to think on your feet, though. It's wise to remember that this time I know you for what you are.'

'You have a child, Holden,' she said, in such a low voice that she could hardly discern it herself, and he had to lean forward to hear. 'A daughter.'

For the first time she saw genuine shock on his face, and before the shock could give way to anything else, she continued in the same low, hurried voice, lowering her eyes. 'And she's ill with leukaemia. She needs an operation, a bone marrow transplant. You're her only chance. That's why I'm here.'

CHAPTER FIVE

THERE was a long silence, during which she didn't have the courage to raise her eyes to his face.

'Is this some kind of joke?' he asked quietly.

She said, in the same semi-audible voice, 'No joke. After you left, after we broke up, had that argument, I carried on working on the liner for another two months. At first, when my period was late, I didn't even notice. My periods had always been as regular as clockwork and I knew, when we had made love, that there was no chance that anything could happen. Then I started to feel sick.' She took a sip from her glass and licked her lips nervously, still not daring to meet his eyes. Actually, she was feeling pretty sick at the moment, but having thrown him that shocking revelation, she knew that she had to give him some details of what had happened. 'I knew that it couldn't be sea-sickness, even though I tried to convince myself that that was the explanation, but then I went to see the ship's doctor and she, well…she said that my cycle might have been disrupted originally by the change in the time zones between England and the Caribbean, or by the stress of taking on the job. She said that it was bad luck. Bad luck!'

'My God.'

She looked at him from under her lashes to find that the shock still hadn't worn off. He looked like a man who had been slugged by something very hard, very large, and very unexpected. That, she thought uneasily, didn't make her feel any better.

At the time, she had fleetingly considered telling him about the pregnancy, but then she had thought about the possible consequences of doing any such thing. At the very least, he would probably accuse her of exploiting a situation to collect hefty maintenance, and at the worst he might try and take the baby away from her. After all, she was young and without a job while he had all the money at his fingertips to persuade the courts that his child would be better off living with him.

But the thought that she had kept his child a secret from him had never stopped nagging away at her conscience, however much she told herself that she had taken the only real option open to her, which had been to throw herself on her aunt's mercy and carry on with her life as best as she could.

'I know this must be something of a shock...'

She finally looked at him and started back when she saw the raw anger in his clenched face.

'Something of a shock? No. Why should it be something of a shock? Isn't it every day that a woman strolls into your office and informs you that you have a child?'

He stood up and she watched him worriedly.

'Where are you going? What are you doing?' There was panic in her voice. He wouldn't walk out now, would he? Not when he knew the situation? Not when he knew that the life of his child was depending on him?

'I can't talk here,' he said tautly, his eyes violent. 'I have an apartment close to Knightsbridge.'

'But...' She began to protest, only to realise that he was walking away, expecting her to follow him, and she hurriedly stood up, half running to keep up with his long strides.

He had tossed some money on the table before leaving, and she saw the waiter hurry to collect it, counting the notes, thinking about racing after him to give him his change. He didn't have the chance, though. She could barely keep up with him.

He called for a taxi as soon as they were outside, and as soon as they were inside she turned to him, her face anxious.

'I'm sorry,' she said, and the apology met with a swift, angry response.

'Your sorrow, your apologies, are beside the point now.'

'What else was I supposed to do?' she asked, with a flare of anger now.

His profile was sharply silhouetted against the window. He raked his fingers through his hair and when he spoke it was in a more controlled voice.

'Let's not go into a long post-mortem,' he said. 'Tell me about her.' His voice was ragged.

'Her name is Harriet,' Marie said. 'We call her Hattie.' She smiled. 'She has dark hair and blue eyes, and…' How to summarise nearly three years into a sentence? She could spend a month, a year, and she wouldn't be able to cover everything. This, she thought with a pang, was what he had missed out on. 'And she's very clever,' she finished a little lamely.

She stole a glance at him and looked away. If he disliked her three years ago, after that harrowing argument that had ended all her dreams, then he hated her now. He hated her for having kept his child a secret.

'How could you keep this from me?' he asked, looking at her savagely. 'Would you ever have informed me that I had fathered a child if my help wasn't needed? Damn you!' She could see that he was fighting to keep his anger on a leash. 'What's wrong with her?' He had his voice under control now, but there was nothing gentle in his expression. 'Is she…?'

'She's not a well little girl,' Marie murmured, trembling. 'She needs a bone marrow transplant. We're hoping that you will be compatible.' There was an edge of quiet desperation in her voice. How could she explain to him that she had lived with this nightmare, while at least he had been spared that?

'When will I be able to see the consultant?'

'As soon as possible. I'm sorry…'

'If you apologise once more, I'll throttle you!' he ground out. He sat back and closed his eyes.

'I know I've upset your life,' she said. 'I never even asked you whether you're married, whether you have a family of your own.'

'It wouldn't have made any difference,' he said, turning to look at her. 'But I'm not, and I haven't. She's my child! Do you think a wife and two point four children would have made any difference to whether I agreed to this operation or not?'

'Our child,' she corrected. 'And I don't know, do I?'

He threw her a savage look, but refrained from commenting on that remark. 'Where are you living now? What are you doing jobwise?'

'After I returned to England I found myself a job at a local company, in the accounts department. It wasn't what I had hoped for. I had wanted a career, something that used my degree, but I couldn't afford to be choosy. I needed the money, and they were kind enough to keep me on after Hattie was born, even though I wasn't entitled to maternity leave. I was lucky.'

'Lucky? You should have come to me! I was the one

responsible for the welfare of our child! Not some damn local company!'

'Oh, what's the point arguing about this?' she asked wearily. She felt battered. True, she had anticipated his reaction, she had known that he wasn't going to smile and forgive. Forgiveness wasn't an emotion that existed in his repertoire. But she felt as if she were reeling under the weight of something too heavy to shoulder.

The taxi had pulled up outside an expensive block of security-guarded apartments, and she allowed herself to be led up to his suite on the third floor.

She would have to telephone her aunt shortly and let her know what was going on.

He slipped his key into the door and pushed it open, striding inside, and she followed him, shutting the door behind her.

If he hadn't told her that he had never married, she would have guessed it from this apartment. It was very masculine. No female touches anywhere. The furniture was black leather, the decor sparse and expensively functional rather than homely.

'You never told me where you were living,' he said with his back to her. He shrugged off his jacket and she looked at that long, lean body with its aura of power and aggressive masculinity. They had been arguing so vehemently over lunch that she had begun to see him as an opponent rather than a man. Now she looked at him and felt an unwanted shiver of awareness. He poured himself a drink and faced her across the slow, square marble table on which was laid an exotically carved chess set, one of the few non-essential things in the room.

'I haven't told you because I couldn't face another lecture on how I should have come running to you the minute I found out that I was pregnant.'

'Sit down.'

'Stop giving me orders! Sit! Stand! Come here! Go there!'

'Sit down!'

His voice was like a whip and she subsided into one of the leather chairs and glowered at him. How much longer was he going to show the naked face of his antagonism, she wondered? All the aggression and arrogance which she had only glimpsed during their brief, disastrous love affair was in full view now.

She watched him warily as he moved towards her to sit opposite her, and he sighed with impatient frustration. 'Tell me where you're living,' he repeated, with less open hostility.

'With my aunt.'

'I remember you mentioning your aunt,' he said slowly. He rested his elbows on his knees and cradled the glass in his hands. For some reason she felt her mind go blank as she looked at those hands. They touched me once, she thought, and she lifted her eyes quickly because hard on the heels of that thought came another, the memory of her body's powerful response to his. She didn't want to think about that. It threatened to destroy her self-composure. All that, she thought, was in the past, water under the bridge. He hated her now, for more than just being a gold-digger in his eyes.

'Do you?' she asked politely. 'I didn't think you would.'

'I told you—' his eyes narrowed '—I remember everything about you. Why are you living with this aunt, if the two of you don't get along?'

'We didn't,' Marie explained a little reluctantly. It was understandable that he wanted to find out more about her, about her circumstances, but she felt strange, a little frightened, at exposing herself to him.

'But?' he prompted with a hint of impatience. 'Dammit, I'm not prying into your private life for the hell of it! I want to know what kind of life my child has had!'

'Our child.'

His lips thinned and she carried on hastily, 'I was terrified when I returned to England. I had no idea what my aunt was going to say, but I didn't have any choice in the matter. She had to be told. I had nowhere else to live; my life was in a shambles.'

His eyes darkened and she knew what was going through his head. That her life was in a shambles, she was pregnant with nowhere to turn, but anywhere and anyone was better than the man who had fathered her child.

He would never understand that the very reason she had broken off their relationship had been the reason why she could not have thrown herself on his mercy.

He had had no intention of extending their relationship into anything other than a casual fling. It was the way he operated. He didn't want commitment of any nature, and that was what he had told her himself. How would he have reacted if she had shown up on his doorstep, complete with her suitcase and a protruding stomach? It would have proved her to be the conniving little opportunist that he believed her to be, and she had loved him too much to force him into a marriage of obligation. It was all very well for him to tear into her for having kept him in the dark, but he was viewing it from a completely different perspective. Now she was no threat to that free and easy lifestyle he had adopted. She had her own life, she was no longer desperate, lonely and confused.

'I had half expected my aunt to throw me out on my ear, but she didn't. She was pleased! I mean not that my life had been thrown out of joint, that my plans for a grand career would have to be shelved, but because I was going to have a baby. She kept saying how thrilling it would be to have a baby in the house, then she'd catch herself and apologise, but actually it made it all so much easier. I don't think I could have coped if she had been worried or censorious, even though that was what I had expected of her. At the very least! When I landed a job three weeks after I got home, she kept giving me anxious looks, like a mother hen, and telling me that I should be taking it easy.'

'It must have been hard for you all the same,' he said. 'I won't tell you that you should have come to me, that I could have lifted some of the burden from your shoulders.'

'Money isn't everything!'

'But it helps!' he shot back.

Their eyes clashed and she felt another shiver of alarm as her senses picked up that dangerous masculinity that radiated out of him in waves. It was something she had not bargained for. Confronting him would be difficult, she had known that from the very first moment she had made the decision to get in touch with him, but she had not expected to find herself still vulnerable to his latent sexuality, especially when the only reaction he had shown her was one of dislike. She wondered whether it wasn't the situation that was getting to her, rather than him. It was more than likely, she decided.

He didn't look away. His grey eyes glittered and held hers until she looked down at her fingers, disturbed.

'I managed all right, despite the fact that there wasn't a lot of money to go round,' she muttered defensively.

'So how, or rather why, had the dragon aunt changed?' His tone was gentler now, less accusatory.

The dragon aunt. She could remember using that expression three years ago when she had laughingly described her aunt to him. Had he remembered or was his description an uncanny coincidence? He surely couldn't have remembered every word that had passed between them! She had. But then she had been in love with him, she thought bitterly. In love and stricken with the temporary blindness that came with the condition.

'I couldn't work it out at first,' she said, her expression distant, looking back into the past. 'Later it all came out. My aunt had been married briefly, before I was born, but it hadn't lasted. You see, she found out that she could never have children and he couldn't accept that, so he left her, and I guess that's why she became so cold and bitter. When I landed on her doorstep after Mum and Dad died in the car crash, I was already a teenager, a reminder of her own infertility. But a baby. A baby in the house was different. She felt as though she was being given the chance to love a tiny human being from its moment of birth. We became very close.' She looked at him and then asked the question that had been nagging away at the back of her mind ever since she had set foot in his office. 'Your mother—how is she?'

'She had a stroke,' he said shortly, 'about two years ago. She never quite recovered. Has difficulty talking.'

'I'm sorry.'

'I expect we should be leaving soon,' he said, standing up and flexing his arms, and she looked at him with sudden panic.

'We?'

He began walking out of the lounge and she half ran behind him, stopping at his bedroom door abruptly as if all her senses had switched on to red alert, telling her that it would be dangerous to follow.

'We?' she repeated, 'What do you mean, we?'

He began tugging at his tie, with his back to her, and her mouth went completely dry as he began stripping off his shirt, tossing it on to the king-size bed with its red and black cover.

Like the rest of the house she had seen, it was a totally masculine room with a sleek desk by the large window, on which was a computer terminal and a telephone. The only picture in the room was a strange, compelling one of two lovers, abstractly painted in golden browns, their bodies disjointed cubes, very lifeless but at the same time highly evocative.

His back was still to her. She could see the powerful muscles of his shoulders, the narrow waist.

'You're not coming back with me, are you?' she asked in a voice which didn't sound like her own at all, and he turned to her, frowning.

'Of course I am. What did you expect?' He began unbuckling his belt and she looked away. Was he going to get completely undressed in front of her? It was ridiculous that she should be feeling this giddy panic, when they had slept together, when she had had his child, but she did.

'I thought that my consultant might contact you,' she said stammering.

He stopped what he was doing, and his mouth tightened. 'I want to get to know my daughter,' he said grimly. 'Whether you like it or not, I'm going to do that. Don't think that you can erase me from your life as soon as my usefulness is over.'

'I never said that!'

'Then what exactly are you saying?' he asked icily. 'Have you told Harriet about me?'

'Not exactly,' Marie admitted, and he looked as if he were about to explode.

'What!'

'I intended to! I just didn't think that the time was right. She's only a baby!'

'Well, you'll have to revise your little game plan,' he informed her harshly, 'and this time it's going to include me. Step one is I go back with you. Step two is that I meet your aunt. Step three I meet my daughter, as her father!'

He whipped off his belt and unzipped his trousers and she turned away, her face flaming.

'There's no need for you to come. We both live in London, for heaven's sake!'

'I'm coming and you'd better get used to the idea. I intend to spend the night at your place, and then we'll decide where we go from there.'

'You can't do that!' Marie protested, feeling disadvantaged because she didn't want to look at him in a state of undress and talking to the door-post was a bit foolish.

'Watch me, and for God's sake stop standing there with your eyes prudishly averted. We slept together, remember!'

Anger forced her head around to see that he was completely naked apart from a pair of silk boxer shorts. Every nerve, every pulse in her seemed to shift into a higher gear as she took in the lightly bronzed body, the broad, muscular chest tapering to the lean waist and hips, the long, athletic legs. She raised her eyes to find that he was looking at her mockingly, and she went bright red.

'There isn't enough room in my aunt's house,' she informed him, wishing that he would get some clothes on instead of just standing there in a state of semi-undress. 'There are only three bedrooms in her house. She sleeps in one, I sleep in one and Hattie sleeps in one. Where do you propose to sleep? Suspended from the ceiling?'

'You can share your bedroom with Hattie,' he said coolly, then his eyes narrowed and he drawled lazily, 'or else you could share it with me.'

She ignored that. 'It's stupid for you to inconvenience my aunt for no valid reason whatsoever.'

'My daughter is reason enough.'

'You'll see her in due course! I don't intend to hide her away from you.'

'You mean the way you spent the last two odd years doing? How thoughtful of you to have this sudden change of heart, Marie. No, the fact is, I don't trust you. I don't trust you to tell her about me, not if you can help it, and if I'm not around, how do I know that what you do say isn't going to turn her against me?' He wandered across to his wardrobe and extracted a loose-fitting beige shirt, which he unhurriedly put on, looking at her as he did up the buttons very slowly, then a pair of olive green trousers.

'Trust me,' she said, clearing her throat.

'Trust you? Don't make me laugh. You made a fool of me once, then you kept my daughter a secret, and you expect me to trust you?' He laughed and it was a bitter, harsh sound. 'I'd sooner trust Attila the Hun.'

He threw a few things into a tan leather holdall, and she watched him, frantically trying to find another way of convincing him that his presence was unwelcome in her aunt's house. For some reason the thought of being in close proximity with him scared her. When she had decided to see him, she had expected his anger but she hadn't banked on him barging into her life.

Had she really imagined that he would be fobbed off with the occasional visit from his daughter?

He brushed past her, back out into the lounge, expecting her to follow, and follow she did.

'What about your work?' she said. 'You have a job to go to. Have you forgotten?'

'I own the company. I've decided to allot myself a bit of holiday. Satisfied?'

'Well, what about me? I have to go to work!'

'Good. That'll give me more time to get to know Harriet before she has her operation.'

She ground her teeth in helpless frustration. Wasn't this just like him? she thought. She must have been crazy to have forgotten how overbearing he was. Ever since she had told him about Harriet he had taken control, and she had been reduced to running behind him, pleading and trying to regain a little of the composure which had been her mainstay for the past three years.

'Coming?' he had the nerve to ask her over his shoulder, his hand resting casually on the front door, and she stormed towards him with her hands on her hips.

'If you get any angrier,' he said with maddening calm, 'you'll explode.'

'And hopefully make a great deal of mess all over your expensive living-room!' she snapped back, as he opened the front door and stood back to let her through.

He laughed drily. 'When did this temper of yours make an appearance?' he asked. 'You were such a happy-go-lucky thing when I knew you.'

'My happy-go-luckiness evaporated when I found myself thrown into life at the deep end!' she told him, walking towards the lift. She was sick of following him like a lap dog. Let him follow in her wake for once.

'What you mean is you wanted to play the martyr and do it all yourself.' He pressed the button on the lift and faced her. 'I would have helped.'

'I didn't want your help!'

'Then don't damn well go on about being thrown into life at the deep end!'

'Don't shout at me!' she shouted, just as the lift doors opened.

They travelled down to the ground floor in silence. Her head was whirling with confused thoughts. What was her aunt going to say? What was she going to tell Hattie? Hi, sweetheart, meet your father? Why did he have to push her into this now? He should have given her time, time to work things out. Life had been so uncomplicated for the past three years. She had worked hard, looked after her child, never complained even when her money was barely enough to make ends meet.

Now, in the space of a few hours, all her quiet calm had been shattered. She hadn't shouted in anger for as far back as she could remember. Yet here she was, shouting as though it were second nature to her.

'My car's in the underground car park,' he told her, once they were outside, and they walked towards it, still in silence.

It was a sleek black Ferrari which he opened by pressing a button on his key-ring, and she quickly slipped into the passenger seat and slammed her door shut, her body tight as he settled his lean frame into the driving seat and stuck the key into the ignition. He didn't switch it on, though. He turned to her and said in a hard, clipped voice, 'Listen to me, and listen to me carefully because I don't intend to repeat this. You're acting like a child—'

'Me?' Her head swung round to him. 'Acting like a child? I came here to ask you a simple little favour—'

'That,' he said curtly, 'has to be the understatement of the decade.'

'Well, whatever,' she conceded. 'I just didn't expect to have my life taken over!'

'Don't make me laugh,' he muttered grimly. 'My life is the one that's been turned on its head.'

'A thousand apologies,' she said with biting sarcasm. 'Are you talking about your work-life or your love-life?' She really was, she realised, beginning to sound churlish but she couldn't seem to help herself, nor could she help the odd twinge of anger at the thought that he might be seeing another woman. That he probably was, in fact. That, for some reason, just made her want to hit out at him even harder, even though she knew well enough that he was right. She had come back into his life with an unexploded bomb and nothing would be the same for him again.

'Both,' he muttered, starting the engine and reversing out of the space with frightening speed.

She stared straight ahead as he accelerated out of the car park, up the ramp and out on to the traffic-laden street.

'And what is she like?' Marie inquired sweetly. 'An understanding creature, I hope. Understanding enough when you tell her that you have a child. The sort of woman your mother would approve of?'

He threw her a sidelong look from under his thick black lashes.

'My mother hasn't met her,' he said smoothly. 'As for understanding, well, I expect she'll be a little surprised, shall we say, at the sudden change in my domestic situation.'

They were inching along. The road was thick with cars, buses, taxis. This was the worst thing about London, Marie had long ago decided, the feeling of never-ending claustrophobia. At one point she and her aunt had debated leaving, moving to somewhere where the air was cleaner and bits of green grass weren't confined to parks, but that was before Harriet had become ill, and of course now they had little option but to remain in London where the hospital was easily accessible.

She wasn't at all sure of the route back to her aunt's house from here but, after staring perplexed at the first roundabout they arrived at, he asked impatiently for the address and proceeded to manoeuvre the back roads as if he had driven to her house a thousand times.

'I've lived in London for most of my adult life,' he said drily, when she expressed surprise, and she said, still bemused, 'So have I.'

'You haven't got much of an adult life behind you, Marie,' he murmured with a flash of sudden amusement, slanting a sideways look at her.

'I feel as though I have,' she admitted. 'Sometimes I feel a hundred.'

He smiled at that, his profile relaxed, and she was suddenly and disturbingly swept back to the time when those lazy, charming smiles were all for her, and the air between them wasn't taut with tension.

'Having a baby must have catapulted you into adulthood,' he commented. 'Did you resent it?'

'Never,' she replied honestly. 'Although I've been living on a knife's edge ever since Hattie was diagnosed. You know, you never think that *your* child might be seriously ill. You always imagine that that happens to other people, people you read about in magazines or newspapers.'

There wasn't as much traffic on these smaller roads, although the pavements were still crowded. She stared out of her window, absent-mindedly watching the pedestrians, wondering where they were all going, heading off to all their various destinations. Where would Holden be going now if she hadn't barged into his life? she wondered. Out with a woman? Her eyes flicked across to him and she

tried to imagine what this woman looked like. Was he
serious about her? She would rather die than ask, because
she didn't want to risk him thinking that she was interested in him.

And she wasn't, she told herself. Not any longer. He
was a part of her past, unavoidably swept up into her
present through circumstances, but she was over him. It
had taken long enough. For months after she had left the
cruise behind her, cutting all ties with the people she had
known there, partly because time had seemed to flash past
her at the speed of light, and partly because she didn't
want any reminders of that other time, he had preyed on
her mind. He had haunted her every waking moment and
quite a few of her sleeping ones as well. She had seen
him in every tall, dark-haired man striding away from her
on the Underground, heard his voice in every distant conversation, only to glance around to find that she was mistaken.

In the end she had had to push the memories away
every time they floated up to the surface and eventually,
once Hattie had been born and her life had changed
course, she had thought that she had conquered them.

After nearly forty minutes, she began to recognise the
streets. They weren't far from the house now, and her
stomach clenched in nervous anticipation.

Hattie would be at home with her aunt, probably having
her tea. They would be chatting and laughing and her aunt
would be trying all sorts of ways of encouraging her to
eat some of her food.

There had been times recently when, under the brave
face, she had longed desperately for him to be there with
her, sharing her agony and anxiety. Her aunt was kind
and sympathetic but she had wanted the father of her
child. Those thoughts had never been conscious ones, she

realised. They had filtered across her mind like intangible but persistent shadows and it was only now, with him sitting there next to her, that she realised how powerful the yearning had been. That disturbed her. What did it mean? She was over him, she knew, wasn't she?

'Which house?' he asked, breaking into her thoughts, and she pointed to the one at the end. White gate, small handkerchief-sized front garden, front door in dire need of repainting.

It was difficult finding parking directly in front and he had to pull into a space further along, edging his car in swiftly. He killed the engine and turned to her, one hand still resting idly on the gear stick.

'I know what you're going to say,' she muttered, with her head averted.

'You're a mind reader now, are you?'

'I can see from the way you looked at this street that you're thinking that it's not up to much. I can tell, I'm not a fool.' She was nervous at the thought of him meeting her daughter and her aunt, and her nerves found their outlet in a show of anger.

'Well, you're doing a damn good impersonation of being one.'

She looked at him, her colour high, expecting to see his mouth drawn into that thin, angry line, but his face was cool and unreadable and for some reason that just made her more angry and tearful.

'I don't want you swanning into my aunt's house and making any derogatory remarks!' she told him, and his face tightened with anger at that. Good, she thought illogically. It was almost better having him angry with her, she could cope with that. When she saw those flashes of humour, though, or sympathy, she felt uneasy deep inside herself, as though somewhere foundations carefully erected over three years were beginning to crack.

'What kind of person do you think I am?' he asked harshly.

'Your mother's son!'

'And what the hell is that supposed to mean?'

'Nothing.' She remembered that overheard conversation as though it were yesterday and blindly pulled at the door-handle, half expecting him to yank her back and demand an explanation for what she had said. Of course, the damn thing wouldn't budge. He had centrally locked the car so she had been struggling with an immovable object.

'Trapped?' he asked mildly, and she turned to him, her face bright red.

'I'm glad you think this whole thing is funny! I'm glad you see it all as a joke!'

His hand snapped out, clasping her arm, and he pulled her towards him.

'It's not funny,' he said grimly, 'and it's no joke.' They stared at each other in silence. His face was so close to hers that she felt as though she were drowning in the depths of his grey eyes. She found that she was holding her breath.

'I know you're nervous,' he told her in a hard, careful voice that made her feel like a recalcitrant child. 'Dammit, don't you think that I haven't got a little bit to be nervous about as well? But getting angry with me isn't going to do any good.'

'I suppose not,' she agreed reluctantly. He was making her tense, looking at her like that, his grey eyes focused and intent. She squirmed a little and he let her go.

'Come on,' she said with a sigh. 'Come and meet your daughter.'

CHAPTER SIX

FAMILIAR teatime sounds greeted her as she opened the front door. Her aunt was making strange noises, emulating a plane or a train or anything that could divert Harriet's attention and allow a mouthful of food to be slipped in. Even as a baby, she had not been an enormous eater. Food had had to be coaxed into her.

Marie smiled to herself, already looking forward to seeing that pretty blue-eyed, doll-like face, framed by curly, short, dark hair.

For an instant she almost forgot about Holden, and she had to catch herself and turn around. He had left his hold-all by the front door and his hands were in his pockets.

'I thought that she'd be in bed,' he said, looking at her. 'You said she was ill.'

'She is,' Marie answered, sobering, 'but she makes the best of it. Children do.'

He walked towards her, long, lean, his natural male aggressiveness tempered by something that she couldn't quite put her finger on. A certain hesitancy perhaps. She badly would have liked to have slipped her arm into his but she restrained the urge. His touch was electric, it did something to her nervous system, and never mind how many times she told herself that he had been cleansed from her system.

The kitchen door was open and she was the first to

appear, smiling as Hattie stood up, her small face beaming.

'She's eaten half,' her aunt said by way of greeting, 'but not without the usual fuss.' There was curiosity in her eyes, and Marie knew that she would be dying to find out how the meeting went but, with Hattie there, she would hold that curiosity in check until later, when they were alone together.

'I'm not hungry any more, Mummy,' Hattie said. 'Did you bring me any presents?' She stepped out from behind the little red table which had been one of Marie's extravagant purchases bought shortly after the high chair had taken up permanent abode in the attic.

'Sort of,' Marie said, glancing at her aunt. She looked over her shoulder, then saw the shock register on her aunt's face.

Holden walked into the kitchen, dwarfing it, his hands still in his pockets. He didn't look nervous, but there was a certain tension in the way he held himself, in his erect back, the stiffness of his jaw.

'Marie,' her aunt said, 'you didn't...'

'She didn't know,' Holden said, his deep voice smooth and with those undertones of persuasive charm which had knocked Marie sideways the first time she had ever met him. 'Mrs...?'

'Palin, Edith Palin.' She had stood up and was staring at Holden as though he had landed from another planet. 'I'll make us a cup of tea, shall I?' she stammered, and Marie nodded.

'Who's that man?' Harriet asked, her blue eyes flicking from her mother's face to Holden's, and then back to her mother's.

'Darling—' she took a deep breath '—he's...'

'A friend,' Holden said. 'My name is Holden

Greystone.' He held out his hand and Harriet eyed it dubiously.

'I'm not allowed to talk to strangers,' she said.

'Quite right,' Holden said gravely, smiling down at Harriet's earnest face.

Edith was busying herself in the kitchen and Marie had to restrain herself from grinning. That back, she thought, spoke volumes.

'Let's go into the sitting-room,' she said to Harriet. 'Need a hand with anything, Edith?' she asked, and her aunt shook her head and began fetching mugs out of the cupboard.

The three of them, Holden, Harriet, herself, went into the sitting-room. We should be a family, Marie thought, instead of two adults caught on opposite sides of a battlefield, with their child in the middle.

Harriet was clinging to her and gazing up at Holden, and Holden's face was inscrutable. He sat down on the sofa and looked around him, but he couldn't get enough of his daughter. Marie could see that from the way his eyes kept returning to her face, as though he had to keep reminding himself of this living proof of his fatherhood.

'I'm nearly three,' Harriet said, unaware of the odd tenseness in the room. 'Mummy's going to give me a My Little Pony and a My Little Pony kitchen for my birthday. Do you have a Little Pony?'

Holden was smiling, his grey eyes oddly gentle. 'No, I haven't. Should I?'

This question seemed to floor her completely and she stood silently watching him, holding Marie's hand.

'Holden's here,' she began, pulling her daughter up on to her lap, 'to help you, because you're ill.'

'I need an operation,' Harriet informed him, stumbling

over the word and finally getting it more or less right. 'Mummy says I can have a plaster on it afterwards.'

'She's fixated with plasters,' Marie explained nervously. 'Darling,' she said to her daughter, stroking her hair, coiling it into a ponytail, then idly plaiting it behind her back, 'we're all hoping that Holden might be able to help make you better.'

'Mummy got cross when I put three plasters on my doll,' Harriet said, losing interest in the subject of her health.

Edith walked in with the tray, deposited it on the coffee-table in the middle of the room, and began pouring tea. She still wasn't quite looking at Holden, and Marie thought that it was a little like a badly executed drama, with poorly trained actors woodenly speaking their lines.

'Come along, Hattie,' Edith said, holding out her hand. 'Bath time. Say bye-bye to Mr Greystone now.'

'I want Mummy to read me a story.'

'I will,' Marie said, smiling, 'after you've had your bath.' This was their usual routine. The coaxing of tea, which could take anything from ten minutes to an hour, the bath which involved an assortment of plastic objects and the bedtime story, which was mostly *Little Red Riding Hood* or *The Three Little Pigs*, which never failed to fascinate her daughter. It was a good routine. She glanced across the sitting-room at Holden, who had stood up as soon as Edith and Harriet were out of the room, and begun prowling, his body graceful but restless.

'Thank you for not telling Hattie who you were,' she said quietly. He didn't answer. 'I'll explain it to her in due course, when the time is right.' Still no response. 'Will you stop pacing?' she asked, bristling a little, 'You're making me nervous!'

'Oh, I am, am I?' he said, moving to close the door to

the sitting-room. 'Well, I wouldn't want to do that, would I?' He raked his fingers through his hair, his grey eyes ferocious.

'I have no idea why you're angry...'

He walked across to her and leaned over, propping himself up by his hands on either side of her chair, and she cowered back nervously.

'You have every idea why I'm angry,' he muttered. 'I feel like a damned intruder here, in front of my own daughter! My own flesh and blood!'

'Yes, well, of course you will,' Marie said in a soothing voice, eyeing him warily from under her lashes and wishing that he would prowl to some other part of the room instead of towering over her so that she couldn't breathe. 'You don't know her.'

'My point exactly,' he said, his voice razor-smooth and cold.

She sighed inaudibly. 'Not this again. Haven't we thrashed this one out enough?'

'No!' he said so sharply that she nearly jumped. 'This whole situation is crazy!'

'I didn't ask you to come here for the night!' she retorted, flushing with angry guilt at the accusation in his voice. 'You do happen to be an uninvited guest!'

He didn't like that. His hand shot out, curling around her wrist, and her laboured breathing became downright uncomfortable. She hated him being so near to her. It made her dizzy and disoriented.

'What a nice feeling, being a guest around your own daughter!'

'There's no point going over this time and time again!' she flared. 'I wouldn't—'

'Mum!' Harriet's voice drifted down the stairs, full of

childish demand, and they both turned to the door, instantly frozen.

'She wants me to read her a story,' Marie muttered. 'So if you see your way to letting go of my wrist...'

'I'll come with you.' He straightened up, stuck both hands back into his pockets and looked at her challengingly.

Marie shrugged in a pretence of not caring one way or another, but she resented the way that he was intruding on her space. Part of her could understand it, but she wasn't about to start paying particular attention to that part.

Those acid words thrown at her by his mother three years ago, and his unjustified accusations, were too firmly embedded in her mind to allow her to bend in sympathy for what he must be going through. As far as his mother was concerned, she thought, I wasn't good enough, I was a little nobody who had to be warned against getting ideas above her station, and as far as Holden was concerned, I was all right for a fling but not worth any kind of involvement, and the minute he thought that I might be after his money, he made no effort to let me explain. Why, she thought rebelliously, should I feel in the least bit sympathetic towards him?

She stood up, not looking at him, and he caught her by her shoulder, turning her around so that she had to face him, and then tilting her head so that she had to focus on that brooding, shuttered face.

'What did you tell her about me?' he asked.

'What are you talking about? I haven't had a chance to speak to Hattie since we arrived!'

'Don't be stupid,' he grated. 'I mean, what did you tell her about her father? Surely you didn't tell her that she was brought by a stork and deposited under a cabbage leaf somewhere in the garden.'

'She's never really asked. She's too young to understand the concept of being the child of a single parent.'

That wasn't strictly true but she wasn't going to inform him of that. Harriet had recently, out of the blue, asked her where her daddy was, because her little friends all had daddies, and Marie had hedged a bit, and the conversation had lapsed.

'How convenient for you.'

'Stop trying to push me into a corner,' she snapped. 'You're here, whether I like it or not, so can't we both just make the best of it?'

There was another 'Mum' call down the stairs, this time bordering on plaintive, and she said hurriedly, 'Are you coming?' and he let her go abruptly, nodding, and she turned away and walked quickly up the stairs, hotly aware of him behind her.

She had remembered so much about him, but, as she was realising, she had forgotten an equal amount. She had forgotten how disturbing his presence could be. She had remembered, from that last encounter between them, how alarming he could be, but time had dulled the edges of the memory, and alarming now seemed like a huge, laughable understatement. He was darkly menacing, dangerous and unfathomable.

Her aunt's house was small. Every square inch of space was utilised. Out of the corner of her eye, she could see the one bathroom with its array of childish clutter, the plastic toys neatly stacked along the edge, and Harriet's bedroom always, however many times it was tidied, seemed to be in a state of semi-permanent disorder. She thought of Holden's massive, expensively furnished apartment and her lips tightened.

'Thanks, Edith,' she said to her aunt, smiling at her, 'I'll take over from here.'

Her aunt nodded and shuffled past Holden, half shutting the door behind her.

As in the kitchen, his presence filled the room and took it over, and she could see Harriet looking at him, her eyes huge.

'We're going to read you a story,' Marie said, sitting on the edge of the bed, and not looking at him, though very much aware of him close behind her.

There was a little blue lamp on the chest of drawers next to the bed, and as he moved round to sit next to her his face was thrown into angular shadows.

'What's it to be tonight, sweetie?' she asked, tearing her eyes away from him and giving herself a mental shake. What was wrong with her, for heaven's sake? '*The Three Little Pigs*, or *Little Red Riding Hood*?' Once upon a time there used to be a book, but after what seemed like several hundred tellings, Marie no longer needed it. She could trot out either story and bet that it was near word-perfect.

'I know another one,' Holden said casually, and in the shadowy light she could almost see her daughter being mesmerised by him. She felt a strange rush of panic and had to force it back.

'You do?' Harriet asked in a whisper, and he nodded.

'*The Elves and the Tailor*,' he murmured.

'Shoemaker,' Marie automatically corrected, and he raised one eyebrow and glanced at her.

'Different story.'

'Of course,' she agreed drily.

'It's about the shoemaker's brother,' he began, and after five minutes Harriet was fascinated. She was still way too young to question the coincidence of little elves appearing

on the doorstep of the same family, and she listened en-
raptured to the telling of his version of the tale.

By the time she was drowsily beginning to fall asleep,
she was well on the way to deserting the I-don't-know-
you camp in favour of the I-like-you camp and Marie felt
torn by conflicting emotions. An odd antagonism towards
Holden that he was creeping like a stealthy thief into her
life and taking over her child, and relief that his meeting
with his daughter had not been as anxious as she had
expected.

She kissed Harriet before leaving the room, and noticed
that he simply murmured, 'Goodnight,' before following
her out.

'She's stunning,' he said in a low murmur, as they
walked down the stairs.

Marie smiled. 'Do I hear a hint of parental pride in that
statement?' she asked, glancing at him. It was different
somehow having him say that, as opposed to anyone else
saying it. It made her feel oddly pleased.

'Of course, she looks like me,' he said in a contented,
teasing voice, returning her glance.

'Of course,' Marie conceded, 'and she's bright too.'

'My genes.' There was a moment of truce so perfect
that it made her catch her breath.

Edith was in the kitchen clearing away Harriet's tea,
and she turned to Holden, wiping her hands on her apron.

'Will you be staying to dinner, Mr Greystone?'

His eyes flickered towards Marie and then he said,
'Yes, I will. I think, if I may, that I'll grab a shower. Is
that OK?'

She nodded silently, looking down. Had he always
made her feel so self-conscious, so ready to go into battle?
she wondered. Not when they had first met, she knew that
much. Then she had felt warm, free, wildly in love. A lot

of bitterness has accumulated over the years, she thought, that's why I feel like this now. There had been a moment just then, a fleeting instant, when they had shared an absolute harmony, but it had been Hattie who had linked them. Without her, there were too many bitter memories for them ever to surmount.

As soon as he had left the kitchen, her aunt turned to her and Marie grinned ruefully.

'What could I do?' she asked, answering the unspoken question. 'I told him about Hattie, and he went mad.' She sat down at the kitchen table and her aunt sat opposite her.

'Shock, I expect,' she murmured. 'Is he here to stay?'

Marie lifted her eyes, startled. 'Of course not! He insisted on staying tonight because he wanted to meet Hattie, but tomorrow he'll be off. I shall visit the consultant, and I can get in touch with him when the time comes.'

'He doesn't look like the kind of man who's going to go away easily,' her aunt commented. 'Not if he doesn't want to.'

'Of course he's going to go away,' Marie said uneasily. 'He has his own place. He can't stay here indefinitely. He wouldn't want to. He has his big flat, his big bed.' She was twiddling her fingers together, and her aunt held her hands firmly in her own.

'You have to think of Hattie,' she said, and Marie opened her mouth to protest that that was all she had ever done, but before she could utter one syllable, her aunt continued in the same flat, gentle voice, 'You've managed well these past few years. We both have. But now that he's back in your life, you're not going to be able to brush him under the carpet. He'll want to see Hattie, and he has a right.'

'Why?' Marie asked with hostility, but her words sounded weak and there was impotent anger in her voice.

'Because he's her father.'

'He fathered her, you mean,' she said fiercely. 'There's a difference. He never wanted me as anything more than a temporary sleeping companion. His mother thought that I was beneath him, and so did he, and he never even doubted that he might be wrong when he accused me of being after his money. So why should he have any rights?'

'Because,' her aunt said with an illogicality which Marie could follow only too well, 'he has.'

She stood up and said briskly, 'What shall we cook? I had chops, but only two. What do you think?'

'I think we should have the chops, and he can have whatever he likes in whatever restaurant he chooses. He has a girlfriend. Let him take her out.'

Her aunt turned towards her, her eyes narrowed. 'Not jealous, are you, Marie Stephens?'

Marie laughed. Jealous? What an idea! 'Why should I be?' she asked brightly. 'What we had is in the past! In fact, he rubs me up the wrong way, if you want to know.'

'Is that a fact?'

'Yes,' Marie said with a hint of defiance, 'it most certainly is a fact.'

'What is?' He startled them both, appearing in the doorway, his hair still damp and combed back from his face. He had changed into a fresh shirt, a faded blue one, and a pair of jeans. She had, she realised, never seen him in jeans before. He looked long and lean and incredibly attractive. Because she could see her aunt watching her speculatively out of the corner of her eye, she plastered a polite smile on her face and said blandly, 'We only have two chops. In other words, there isn't enough food to feed the starving thousands never mind three of us.'

'Marie!' her aunt exclaimed.

'You mentioned a woman in your life. Please don't feel that you have to stay here and eat with us.' She hated the demon in her that still wanted to hurt him after all this time, when indifference should have been the only emotion she felt in his presence. She had given herself to him once, and she had learned a bitter lesson. Nothing had changed since then, apart from the arrival of her beloved daughter on the scene. He still considered her beneath him and his accusations hurled at her three years ago still summed up how he essentially felt about her.

Holden's mouth tightened but he didn't say anything. Her aunt began setting the table, laying out three places, and he reached out to give her a hand.

Nothing like making yourself at home, is there? Marie thought sourly. His action had surprised her aunt, but she had willingly handed him the table mats and pointed to where the plates were kept, and they began chatting about nothing in particular, while she seethed in silence on her chair.

'Why don't we have a takeaway?' he asked, and her aunt responded immediately by agreeing. That made Marie even more sour. She was beginning to feel like an ill-mannered child in her own house, which was ridiculous.

'I've got a menu card somewhere,' her aunt said, frowning. 'I'll just go and see if I can dig it up. Marie and I don't often have takeaways.'

'No,' Marie said loudly, taking over her aunt's job of putting glasses on the table. 'We can't afford such luxuries.'

That made her aunt open her mouth as if she were about to say something, but she changed her mind and left them in the kitchen while she began searching upstairs for the

elusive menu. Marie could hear the creak of the floor-
boards, then rustling as drawers were rummaged through.
She still wasn't looking at Holden. She was being stupid,
acting like a child instead of an adult, but he made her
edgy and angry.

'And what is that supposed to mean?' he asked with
ice in his voice, and she shrugged, keeping her eyes studiously averted. If she didn't look at that muscular body,
if she didn't see those glinting grey eyes or the warm
curve of his mouth, then she could easily pretend that he
wasn't having any effect on her.

'It's not supposed to mean anything,' she returned in a
sugary voice. 'I was simply stating a fact. Edith and I
don't have a great deal of money for life's little luxuries
and it's no good your trying to buy your way into her
affections, or Hattie's for that matter, by throwing your
money around.'

He came round the table so quickly and silently that
she was barely aware of him doing it until he was holding
her by her shoulders and pinning her against the kitchen
wall.

'Now you listen to me,' he ground out, 'I'm not about
to start buying my way into anyone's affections. There
wasn't enough food, so I suggested an alternative.'

'I can think of another option,' she snapped back,
breathing hard. 'It's called leaving. You open the front
door, you walk through the front door, you close the front
door behind you, you find a meal somewhere else.'

'I'm here,' he said tightly, 'and I'm not about to oblige
you by leaving. And look at me when I'm talking to you!'

She raised reluctant brown eyes, her expression half
sulky, half angry.

'Oh, all right,' she said. 'I'm not about to start World
War Three in here over whether we have a takeaway or

not.' She had hoped that that would do the trick and he would release her, but it didn't. He continued to stare at her and she found that she couldn't look away.

The atmosphere had changed between them. She didn't quite know why or how, because there was still dark, brooding anger stamped on his face, but it had. She suddenly felt very hot, very conscious of her body, and she wriggled against his hands, which only had the opposite effect of making him push her a little harder against the wall.

It seem an eternity before his grip slackened, but of course it wasn't. It was a matter of seconds, and when she could have pushed him away quite easily and found refuge in some other part of the kitchen, she didn't. Her limbs seemed to have become lead weights, anchoring her to the ground, and her breasts were aching.

'Were you really just after my money?' he asked, and she had to think a little before knowing what he was going on about. She still pretended to misunderstand though, giving him a puzzled look which made his black brows snap together impatiently.

'Don't tell me I was the object of some damned bet which you decided to call off. I spent a long time, too damned long, thinking about that and I don't believe I could have been that wrong about you. I know what I heard but it's preyed on my mind, over and over and over. You weren't the sort of girl who plays games like that.'

'Let me go.'

'Not until you've answered me!'

'Why? What's the point? Why it ended between us doesn't change the fact that I had a baby by you, that she's ill, and that you're here now.' Her voice was unsteady, which was appropriate because the rest of her felt quite unsteady as well.

'Answer me!'

'Why should I? You couldn't have felt anything for me one way or the other if you found it so easy to jump to all the wrong conclusions about me.'

'What did you want me to feel for you?' he asked, and her lips tightened. No way, she thought, no way am I ever going to be vulnerable again.

'Nothing,' she said. 'We were mismatched, it was a mistake.'

'Yet look at what came of that mistake.' His eyes darkened.

'That's not fair,' she muttered. 'Hattie is my life, my sun, my stars, my whole world. You wouldn't be here now if it weren't for her!' She looked at him defiantly, but inside she felt confused and bewildered because she felt complete now that he was here, and she didn't want to feel complete in his presence, she didn't want to find herself depending on him. Bitterness, when it takes root, is hard to destroy.

'Are you finished?' she asked tightly.

'Not yet,' he murmured, his voice husky, and before she could move to avoid him his mouth descended over hers, driving her back. This wasn't like that angry kiss in the wine bar. There was no tenderness in it, but there was passion and the sort of hunger which Marie had forgotten existed. For a fraction of a second, her lips moulded to his and their tongues clashed and squirmed against each other, sending waves of desire through her.

Then sanity returned and with it horror at what she had allowed her body to do. She pushed at him and he fell back, breathing heavily, his eyes dark and hot as though live coals were burning behind them.

'I don't want you to ever touch me again!' she said, talking in a soft voice but one which was suffused with appalled anger. She shuffled out of his reach and he spun around to face her.

'Why?' he mocked. 'Because you're so indifferent to me? Because you can't bear me to be near you?'

'That's right!'

'Then you'd better inform your body of that because, from what I've just seen, it thinks otherwise.'

His lips curled into a smile, and if she were standing any closer she would have slapped him. Instead, she closed her fists and took a couple of very deep breaths.

'You disgust me,' she said, backing as he took one step forward, his face hard, and every muscle in him speaking of a threat that frightened her.

'You have a girlfriend,' she said, clutching at anything to stop him from coming any closer to her. After years in cold storage, she had thought herself well and truly beyond reach of this kind of foolish emotional response, but she had been wrong. She had to face the fact that she was as aware of him as a man as she had ever been, even though she would fight that awareness tooth and nail. When he had touched her, her whole body had gone up in flames, and for an instant rational thought was lost under a tidal wave of desire.

The realisation horrified her. She had backed away from him once because she had seen in their relationship the promise of hurt, and she doubted that anything had changed since.

'So I have,' he agreed smoothly, still advancing on her. 'But in the space of twenty-four hours my life has been changed, and I don't think that that particular relationship can survive the upheaval.'

Marie thought of that nameless, faceless woman and felt a sudden pang of sympathy. Had she been foolishly nurturing dreams that Holden Greystone was the one true love of her life? she thought bitterly. Just as she herself had?

'It was never serious between us,' he said, reading her face. 'She won't be broken-hearted. Who knows, she might even be relieved.'

'What do you mean?'

'Rebecca has slowly realised that I'm a lost cause and she's way too smart to stick around and fight for a lost cause. She wants a commitment I could never give her. We've been drifting apart for weeks now, and when I tell her about this—' he hesitated and shot her an odd look '—she'll leave with only a few regrets.'

So he was still fighting commitment, she thought bitterly. He'll never change, will he?

They heard footsteps descending and a rush of relief washed over her. He saw it and his eyes narrowed.

'We're not through yet,' he murmured, and something in the way he said that sent a shiver of apprehension running down her spine, then her aunt wandered into the kitchen with the green menu card in her hand.

'Found it,' she said triumphantly, looking at Marie. 'Upstairs in the toy box on the landing. It's been used as a drawing board for Hattie, but I think we can just about manage to discern a few dishes.'

Marie was still shaking from what had just taken place. She managed a weak smile and then thankfully her aunt's attention was diverted by Holden, who strolled over to read the menu, his voice back to its normal, velvety charm as he began discussing what they could eat, how far the takeaway place was, whether it was easy to find; and if there was any tension in the room it evaporated, leaving Marie with the uncomfortable feeling that perhaps she had over-reacted to everything.

What had he meant when he had said that they weren't

through yet? The thought raged in her head, while her mouth smiled and contributed to the conversation. She only realised how tense she was when he had left the kitchen to fetch the food, and the front door had slammed behind him. Then she sat down, her face flushed.

'Whatever is the matter?' her aunt asked, concerned, and Marie rested her head against the palm of her hand. She felt feverish and, while she would have liked to believe that the onset of a cold was the cause of her symptoms, she was forced crossly and hopelessly to push aside any such wishful thinking.

'Nothing,' she mumbled.

'It hurts, does it? His being back in your life when you had convinced yourself that you were well rid of him?'

Marie nodded wearily and her aunt said, 'I know. When Tom walked out, it left a great gaping hole inside, and I have no idea what I would have done if he had turned up years later.' She paused for a moment, lost in unhappy thought, then said briskly, 'I assume his presence here means that he has agreed to have the blood test to find out whether he's a suitable match for Hattie?'

'Mm,' Marie confirmed. 'There was no hesitation. I shall phone Dr Hilburn tomorrow and get things moving along.' Somewhere at the back of her mind, she thought, 'And then things can get back to normal,' but she dismissed that thought with a wave of despair. How would things ever get back to normal when Holden Greystone, like it or not, was now going to be a permanent feature in her life, popping up at regular intervals to visit his daughter? She faced the prospect of having to come to terms with the eventuality of his getting married in due course, of having children of his own, by the right woman, of course. It was a nightmare.

She began chatting about their meeting, giving her aunt

an edited version of what had been said, and omitting that awful point when he had pulled her against him and kissed her, assuming that she had returned to offer herself for sale.

Gradually some of the wound-up tension began to ease out of her, and by the time he returned with the two white plastic carrier bags with their little silver containers she was feeling far more in control of herself. She had had time to slap down her wayward thoughts and to put everything in perspective. He might be back, but hopefully everything would work out with Hattie—the possibility of its not doing so was one which she refused to contemplate—and once her daughter was back on her feet, then she, Marie, could always see to it that she was absent when he called round to visit. With a bit of forward planning, she needn't, she decided, have much to do with him at all. She could carry on with her life and eventually she would meet a man, a nice, uncomplicated man, and she would be able to put the spectre of her past behind her.

Over the Chinese meal, which tasted delicious but which Marie knew, from experience, would leave her with a slight headache the following morning, Holden devoted his attention to Edith. He hardly glanced in Marie's direction at all, and when he did his eyes were unfathomable.

He had, it transpired in conversation, acquired two further cruise liners, a major enterprise which he spoke of in terms of a little hobby, and magnanimously invited them, with Hattie, to use whichever one they chose, whenever, to whatever destination they liked, all free of charge. Her aunt looked interested but Marie murmured a very cool, very polite, 'I don't think so,' which made him look at her with narrow-eyed coldness.

'Why not?' he asked bluntly, then he said, watching

ıer from under his thick lashes while he continued to
manipulate his noodles with his chopsticks. 'There was a
ime when you were very fond of the high seas.'

There was double meaning behind that. She could sense
t even if it managed to go over her aunt's head.

She gave him a smile which was hardly more than a
light twitch of her lips. 'Those days are gone,' she said.
I have a child now. My tastes have changed, and frankly
here's no way that I would want to recapture the past.'

She promptly changed the subject and began talking
bout her plans for the following day. She would phone
ıe consultant, she told Holden, and she hoped that the
lood test could be done as soon as possible.

'I shall come with you,' she said, and he nodded, un-
erstanding her need to be there at every stage of the
rocess that would, not should but would, culminate in
ıe successful transplant of bone marrow for her daughter.

They cleared away the dishes, and for the first time she
ılt relaxed and at ease with him, discussing Hattie, the
ıplications of her illness, the implications of any oper-
ion on both Holden and the little girl.

Various doctors had explained about the illness, and
Iarie herself had devoured any literature she could get
ır hands on about it. They strolled into the lounge with
ıps of coffee and she mostly did the talking while he
ıd her aunt listened.

She was hardly aware when her aunt retired, after an
ıur, to read in her bed. She had become carried away
lking about the thing, the awful thing, that had preyed
ı her mind for what seemed like a lifetime.

'She has to get better,' she told him, looking at that
ırk face across the width of the small room.

'She'll get better.'

'Do you really believe that?'

He nodded. 'Of course I do. You're afraid, I know, but she'll be all right.'

She gave him a hopeful, despairing look and felt a strange comfort that she was sharing this problem with him. Hattie's blood was his blood too, and no one else could share her worries the way he could.

'Fear is a terrible thing,' she whispered, voicing thoughts that had never been voiced before. 'It eats into you and after a while you build your life around it until you're going to go mad. Hattie had always been delicate, and then she developed an infection that quickly became serious. I took her to the hospital, but you never think…do you?' She raised helpless eyes to his.

'No, you don't,' he said seriously. 'But hope can be as strong as fear, and that's what must guide us both now.'

It was close to midnight by the time they finally retired. He was, she admitted, staring upwards at the ceiling, a good listener, and she had needed someone to whom she could pour her heart out. No, she thought with a small frown, she had needed him.

He was back in her life and her aunt had not been far wrong when she had said that he had a right to be a fully fledged, paid-up member of his daughter's life, even if he had been absent for the past three years, because he just had.

And that scared her.

CHAPTER SEVEN

THE following few days were an exercise in self-control. The blood tests had been done and the waiting for results began. That, Marie knew from experience, was by far the worst. It was living on a knife's edge, constantly torn between hope and despair. She returned to work, but concentration was difficult.

'You're terrified, aren't you?' Holden had asked, as they had strolled out of the hospital after his blood had been taken, and she had rounded on him with an anger born out of anxiety and fatigue.

'What do you think? You lashed out at me for not having told you about the pregnancy, but at least you were spared Hattie's illness! The treatments, the misery. Don't forget I know what it's like to watch her deteriorate under that cheerful baby face, and to have blood taken, to wait, only to find out that you're not compatible! Of course I'm damn well terrified!'

He had looked at her grimly, on the point of debating the issue, then he had shaken his head wearily.

'Look,' he had said, 'there's no point in worrying yourself to death. That's not going to be of much use to Hattie, is it?'

'Nor is breezing along pretending that everything's all right! And don't tell me what will be of use to Hattie and what won't! I have three years' experience up on you!'

'Which,' he had shot back, his face flushed with anger,

'is nothing to be proud of!' He had pulled her towards him, his fingers digging into her wrist. 'Listen to me very carefully, Marie Stephens. I'm going to be abroad for a couple of days, until the results come through. The consultant will telephone me as soon as they're received. Enjoy your life as you know it while you can, because when I return things are going to change.'

It had hardly been a pleasant note on which to part company, but she hadn't expected pleasantness to be a part of their relationship. In a way, she was terrified to let it.

She couldn't tell him that enjoying her life as she had known it was now an impossibility. How could she fall back into any kind of routine when thoughts of Hattie were fast becoming entwined with thoughts of him?

Thinking about it now, it amazed her that she had never considered what impact his reappearance in her life would have. She had naïvely assumed that three years would have immunised her against any effect he could have on her senses. She had reckoned on his anger, but she realised now that she had never really considered anything beyond that. He had been a shadow, playing along to her tune, retreating as soon as his usefulness was over.

The bus dropped her off at the corner of the street, and she automatically hopped off, still frowning and thinking.

All those years ago she had shoved his memory into the background because that was the safest place for it. When she and her aunt had discussed getting in touch with him, she had pulled out the memory, dusted it down and decided that it no longer threatened her. She had been an utter fool.

She was still frowning and thinking when she looked up and saw her aunt waving at her, waving madly, and grinning just as madly, and Marie began to run. The results! The results were back! She had not expected the call until later in the evening. Her aunt was grinning, and hope surged through her with a rush that made her feel sick and dizzy. Hope is a dangerous thing, she told herself shakily, but she couldn't push it away. It was as strong as fear, Holden had told her, and it was what must guide them now, and she had been clinging to it with the desperation of a drowning person clinging to a lifebelt.

'Good news,' Edith said, and close up Marie could see that her eyes were watery and red-rimmed.

'Holden's blood...'

'The consultant just phoned fifteen minutes ago. Come inside. Hattie's playing at Emily's house so we can talk without interruption. My dear—' she hustled Marie through the door, and now Marie saw that her aunt's hands were trembling '—Dr Hilburn spoke to me himself. The blood is an excellent match.'

'This isn't a dream, is it?'

'No dream, my dear. The doctor didn't want to raise our hopes, but the operation's been scheduled for the day after tomorrow, and the chances of success are good, those were his exact words, and you know, don't you, that by good he means fantastic!'

'I need to sit down.' Her aunt led her to the kitchen table, poured her a cup of strong, sweet tea and they looked at each other in silence.

'I feel as though I don't dare believe it,' Marie whispered, close to tears.

'Holden should have been informed by now.'

'It's like a dream.'

'You're not going to faint on me, are you?' her aunt asked crisply, smiling and brushing a tear from her cheek, and Marie smiled back.

'I shall try not to.'

The telephone buzzed from the lounge, and Marie jumped up to answer it. Her first thought was, what if it's the doctor and he's phoning to tell me that it's all been a mistake? They read the wrong results.

It wasn't. It was Holden. His deep, aggressive voice sent a shockwave through her, rendering her speechless for a few seconds, then normality returned and she said quickly, 'Have you been told?'

'Yes. Look, I can't talk to you on the phone. I'm at my place. Come.'

Through the euphoric haze, she felt herself bristle at the command in his voice. She had had two weeks to think about him, two weeks to think how the wheel was turning full circle, carrying her back to the place she had thought she had left behind for good, the place where his powerful image ruled her world and no thought was completely free from thoughts of him. She wouldn't let that wheel turn any further, she wouldn't let herself forget the past.

'What for?' she asked. 'I can't.'

'You know my address. I shall expect you within the hour.'

She heard the click as he dropped the receiver, and then the dull, monotonous hum of the dialling tone, and she stared at the phone angrily. How dare he!

'That was Holden,' she told her aunt, walking back into the kitchen and gulping down the remnants of her tea. 'He wants me to meet him at his place.'

'He wants to talk things over with you, I expect,' her aunt said placidly. 'Hattie won't be back for another couple of hours. She's having tea with Emily.'

Marie opened her mouth to inform her aunt that she had no intention of jumping to Holden Greystone's demands, then decided against it. She would go and she would try to hide her antagonism, but only until after the operation. Then, if he thought that he could run her life for her, he was in for a shock.

She hurriedly changed into a pair of jeans and a jumper, called a cab, and spent the thirty-five minutes to his place fuming.

She rang his doorbell, her eyes widening when he pulled open the door wearing a pair of boxer shorts and nothing else.

'You could at least have got dressed,' she said huskily, looking away from the broad, bronzed shoulders, the flat, hard planes of his stomach, the narrow waist.

He raised one eyebrow. 'You're quicker than I thought,' he drawled, walking away and leaving her to shut the door behind her.

She followed him, feeling awkward. He walked across to the bar, poured them both a glass of champagne and held hers out to her.

'Good news, don't you think?' he asked with a slow smile. 'Has it put your terror in abeyance for the time being?'

Marie took a sip from her glass and relaxed a bit.

'Wait here,' he said, 'I'll be back in a few minutes. I'll just get changed.'

He vanished in the direction of his bedroom, and she sat down on the edge of one of the chairs, her arms on her knees, her fingers twiddling with the stem of the glass.

She would stay here, she decided, for half an hour at the most. Enough time to sort out the details of what lay ahead. Then she would get home. There was a lot to be done. A bag would have to be packed for Hattie and, more importantly, she would have to sit her daughter down and explain about the operation. In a way, it was good that she was not even three years old. Fear of the unknown had not yet sunk its teeth into her and with any luck that would stand her in good stead when it came to the operation.

Holden walked back in, casually handsome in a pair of silver-grey trousers and a short-sleeved shirt. He looked relaxed and she uneasily thought what a complex individual he was. He could be sharp and biting, but when he wanted he could also be charming and sympathetic, a rock on whom she could lean.

'Have you spoken to Hattie yet about the operation?' he asked, sitting down on the nearest sofa to her and leaning forward slightly. He took a sip of champagne and surveyed her over the rim of his glass.

'Not yet, no. She's staying with a friend for tea. I shall talk to her about it tomorrow morning. I've taken the next fortnight off work. They've been very understanding.'

'How do you think Hattie will feel about the operation? Scared?'

'No,' Marie said slowly, 'apprehensive perhaps, but she's known all along that she would have to have an operation at some point. She's seen a video of what's wrong inside her—' she smiled '—in animated images that would appeal to a child. That helped.'

He cradled the glass in his hands, then said, his eyes flicking to her, 'I thought that we might take her out somewhere before the operation.'

'What?' For some reason the thought of that horrified her slightly. 'Why?'

His lips thinned. 'Why do you think?'

'I don't think that's a good idea,' Marie said, standing up and restlessly walking around the room.

'I want her to get to know me,' Holden said with elaborate patience, 'and I don't need you fighting me every inch of the way.'

'I'm not doing that!' she protested. 'Of course you want to get to know her. I understand that.'

She had had two weeks to get accustomed to the idea of him being a part of his daughter's life, and she had managed to tidy up all the uneven edges which that scenario presented by assuring herself that she could quite easily have only superficial, fleeting contact with him, a 'Hello' when he came to collect her at the front door, and a polite 'Did you have a nice time?' when he dropped her off. It was difficult to think of a 'Hello' and a 'Did you have a nice time?' as leading up to anything remotely threatening.

'She's a part of your life now, and it's no good wondering whether I did the right thing by keeping her a secret from you.' His face darkened and she continued hastily, 'The fact is that I know you'll want to have contact with her after the operation.' Her eyes flickered away at the thought that the operation might not be successful. 'That's fair enough.'

'How noble of you,' he said drily, and she flushed.

'Well, yes, I think so,' she answered, some of her calm disappearing at his tone of voice. 'But perhaps it would be better to leave it until after the operation. Then you could take her somewhere.'

'No.'

'What do you mean, no?' Marie shot him a sulky, hostile glance from under her lashes.

'I mean I want to see her before she has the operation. We could go to a park somewhere. Take a walk, look at the trees, feed the ducks.'

'*Feed the ducks*? You?' The thought of Holden Greystone feeding ducks made her forget her antagonism and she almost laughed at the thought. 'They'd flap away in fright,' she said, and he looked at her from under his lashes.

'Oh, thanks very much. Well, I'll keep away from the ducks, in that case. I'll let you and Hattie do the feeding.'

Marie fought against her reservations, then gave up. What harm would it do? Anyway, he would simply persist until she gave in, she would be steamrollered into acquiescence, so she nodded and sighed, and listened to him tell her where she could meet him and when.

Hattie, of course, was excited and Marie pretended not to notice Edith's reaction, which was one of thoughtful curiosity.

'He insisted,' she hissed the following morning, as they stood at the front door, 'so you can wipe that speculative look from your face.'

Edith laughed. 'My dear, I never asked for any explanations!'

'You don't have to,' Marie said with amused reproof. 'Your face gives the game away.'

'Well, an old woman can't help wondering how three years of bitterness is culminating in a walk in the park. Not,' she added, inspecting her fingers, 'that I don't think it's a good idea.'

'You're a witch,' Marie said affectionately, giving her a peck on the cheek. 'I'm not getting involved with him,' she continued, *sotto voce* because little ears heard a great deal more than you thought, even when you thought their attention was elsewhere. 'What we had is history.'

'Of course it is.'

'I wouldn't get involved with him again if he were the last man on the face of the earth.'

'Of course you wouldn't.'

'You're impossible.' She looked down at Hattie who

was tugging her hand, and allowed herself to be dragged away to the waiting taxi with a last wave to her aunt.

Holden was waiting for them at the entrance to the park, as they had arranged. She looked at him, took a deep breath, and then walked over to where he was standing. Hattie had developed an acute case of shyness and was clutching her, staring up at him silently. He stooped down so that he was at her level and said with a smile, 'Remember me?' She nodded and clutched. 'I've brought you a present.' He looked up at Marie with silent challenge in his eyes. Hattie, though, clutched less.

'A present?' she asked timidly, her eyes flickering up to her mother's.

'Go ahead, sweetie,' Marie said, knowing that she had been put in an impossible situation.

He extracted the present from behind him and produced it with a flourish, and the shyness evaporated into a delighted smile.

'A My Little Pony!' She held it up to Marie. 'And a My Little Pony brush.' She let go of Marie's hand and said to Holden, who was still stooping, 'Thank you.'

He straightened up and stood alongside Marie while Hattie walked in front, brushing the blue mane of hair.

'I don't want a lecture from you on buying my way into her affections,' he muttered, and she said placidly, 'I wasn't about to give you one.'

'I have three years of giving to catch up on,' he informed her with an odd note of defensiveness in his voice, as they walked into the park. 'I had to restrain myself from buying her the entire contents of the toy department,' he said. 'I never realised there were that many children's toys on the shelves. I counted twelve different model dolls that did any number of things.'

Hattie was walking towards the pond with the pony pressed against her dress.

'We're going to feed the ducks,' she said, turning around and staring up at Holden, and he nodded. 'Yesterday Mummy took me to a farm and I fed the chickens.'

'Yesterday?' Holden asked quizzically, and Marie grinned.

'Three months ago, actually. Children can get a bit confused when it comes to chronology.'

'Eggs come from chickens,' Hattie continued chattily, with no evidence of shyness on the horizon. 'And wool comes from sheep, and feathers come from pillows.'

Holden laughed, which didn't seem to disconcert Hattie at all.

'Amazing grasp of language,' he said to Marie, as they neared the pond. 'She's very advanced for her age.'

'A child prodigy, no less,' Marie agreed with amusement, shelving her self-imposed caution. It was such a nice day—too nice, she thought lazily, to spoil with bitterness, and anyway, she wasn't about to spoil Hattie's enjoyment because of Holden Greystone and the way she felt about him.

She had brought some bread with her, and they sat underneath a tree with Hattie patiently waiting for her to crumble the bread into pieces. She held out her tiny palm and her little fingers curled around the crumbs, then she trotted a few yards away and hurled the bread ineffectually a few feet from her and stared at the ducks with openmouthed glee. When she returned, she placed the My Little Pony on the ground and said seriously, 'He's tired. He wants to sleep.'

'Of course,' Holden said with equal solemnity. 'He does look very tired.'

'If a stranger comes, he'll take My Little Pony,' she said anxiously, and Marie smiled.

'I'll make sure no one takes him,' she said, which was a relief to Hattie, who trotted off back to the feeding zone and tried to entice some more ducks with the bread.

Holden was looking at his daughter with fascination, and Marie felt her heart give a little leap.

'This must be very strange for you,' she murmured, not looking at him but feeling his eyes on her as he faced her.

'Of course it is. I haven't been into a park in years, let alone with a three-year-old hell bent on feeding a troop of ducks. I never realised what I was missing.'

Marie glanced at him in surprise.

'Dammit,' he said under his breath, 'you should have told me when you found out you were pregnant.'

'Don't let's start this again,' she said, frowning, and he sighed with angry frustration.

'I'm tired,' Hattie said, approaching them and sitting down in front of Marie.

'I know,' Marie said, glancing at Holden with expressive eyes.

'The ducks told me that they were full up,' she said, resting against Marie. She looked at Holden. 'They live at Old Macdonald's farm,' she explained gravely. 'They had their breakfast there.'

'What did they have?' he asked interestedly.

'Pancakes.' She thought a little more. 'And baked beans.'

He stood up briskly and held out his hand. 'How would you like to go for a walk on my shoulders?' he said to Hattie. 'We could have a look at the trees. I'll tell you what they're called.'

Hattie was looking revitalised at the prospect of that, and Marie gave her a little encouraging push. He squatted

and lifted her on to his shoulders as though she were as
light as a feather, and they trundled off with Hattie's voice
ringing into the distance, 'I know a nursery rhyme about
a tree. Shall I sing it for you?'

Marie watched them with a wrenching sense of loss.
She didn't want to feel this, she didn't want to confront
what she had missed for three years: the comfort and security of a family life. Holden, she reminded herself, was
charming when he was with Hattie, but he still disliked
her. She wasn't going to drop her defences, she wasn't
going to let herself forget what had happened between
them, because their words spoken in anger and born of
suspicion were as true as they were then.

When they returned, she stood up and shook herself
down, and watched as he lifted Hattie from his shoulders.
Hattie smiled at him with something approaching adoration, and Marie felt a lump in her throat.

They drove back to the house with Hattie asleep in the
back, and mostly in silence. When they arrived, Edith
opened the front door and Marie turned to him and said
politely, 'Thank you for a very pleasant day.' She un-
loaded Hattie and was walking towards the front door
when he stopped her.

'Not so fast,' he said, smiling at Edith, bending to tou-
sle Hattie's hair.

'We're going for a little drive,' he said to Marie, standing up and staring at her. 'There's a little matter I want
to discuss with you.'

'Can't it wait?'

'No.' He was still smiling, but there was a rock-hard
implacability to his voice that sent a sort of muted desperation through her. 'Can you spare Marie for a couple
of hours?' he asked Edith, who nodded and tried not to
look openly curious.

'Where are we going?' Marie asked, as soon as they were inside the car, and Holden gave her a swift sideways glance.

'To a restaurant, for lunch.'

'I'm not hungry.'

He ignored her. 'During which we will talk, and behave like civilised adults instead of throwing insults at one another.'

Marie didn't say anything, but her mouth tightened. He was referring to her of course, he was acting as though she had behaved like a child from the minute she laid eyes on him at his office, which simply wasn't true.

The restaurant was on the outskirts of London, a small bistro where Holden appeared to be well known to the manager, well known enough to bypass waiting people and be shown immediately to a corner table amid much joking and long-time-no-see type of remarks. Marie hovered, smilingly politely but inwardly gearing herself up to a confrontation.

'I've had two weeks to think about this,' Holden said, when they had ordered. 'I never saw myself in the role of a father, and I can't say that it hasn't taken some adjusting, but...'

He paused and Marie immediately said, 'Yes, of course. Hattie. I'm prepared to come to some kind of agreement with you as to visiting rights. Every other weekend perhaps. On a Saturday.' Her voice faltered. She hadn't expected a rapturous response to her proposal, but on the other hand, *some* response would have been welcome.

The waiter deposited their drinks on the table and he waited until they were alone again before saying bluntly, 'I'm afraid that's not good enough.' He took a sip from the drink while his eyes skimmed her face.

'I think I'm being very fair,' Marie informed him. 'It

would be too disruptive seeing her during the week. I like to get her to bed early, and God knows what sort of hours you keep at your office. I don't see you swanning off at four to play with your daughter for an hour and a half twice a week!'

The temperature in his eyes dropped from cool to cold. 'Let's get one thing straight,' he said. 'I don't intend to scurry around on a Saturday to take my daughter for a quick walk in the park while you hang around the house, looking at your watch, until I get back. When you decided to get in touch with me, you may have deluded yourself into thinking that I would happily fit in with whatever plans you had for me, but if you did, then you were way off target. That child is a part of my life and she deserves a full-time father, not a semi-stranger she glimpses from time to time.'

'What are you saying?' Marie shot him a confused, dismayed look.

'Hattie is going to live with me.'

'Never!' She leaned forward, trembling. 'You won't take my child away from me! You may think that money buys everything, but you're off your head if you imagine that that includes people.'

'I don't intend to take her away from you,' he said impatiently. 'I'm talking about something altogether more permanent. I've thought this through and I've come up with the conclusion that we must get married.'

She stared at him, open-mouthed, speechless. 'You must be mad,' she said finally.

'Why? It makes sense.'

'To a lunatic perhaps.' Her nerves were jangling and her mouth felt dry. Three years ago she would have given anything to have heard those words but not now, not like this.

The impatience was teetering on the brink of anger, but when he spoke it was with perfect control.

'Hattie needs a family,' he said with relentless logic. 'Look at how she enjoyed the outing to the park.'

'Hattie would have enjoyed an outing to the park if I had gone along with her accompanied by a two-headed alien from outer space.'

'Why don't you stop thinking about yourself and start thinking about our daughter?' His voice was still calm but his eyes were savage.

'How dare you?' she hissed, leaning back to accommodate the waiter who placed their starters in front of them with some panache and then waited tacitly for their reaction, which they both gave while staring at each other in anger.

'You come along,' she spluttered, 'and suddenly you want to take over!'

'I'm not taking over, dammit!'

'No?' She stuck a prawn and ate it, but didn't taste it because she was too busy concentrating on how annoyed she was. 'I'm surprised that you would even consider offering marriage to a gold-digger,' she said bitterly, 'that breed you despise so much.'

He was getting angrier by the minute. She could see it in the tenseness of his jaw and the deliberation of his movements.

'Look,' he said finally, 'there's no point in dragging up the past—'

'The past is part of the present!'

'Hattie is the present! She'll need a family unit even more when she gets out of hospital. How do you think your daughter will feel when she gets older and finds out that you refused to marry her father? When she realises that you denied her a family unit, with all the privileges that money can bring, simply because of your pride?'

'Pride has nothing to do with it! What about love?'

His mouth hardened. 'What about it?'

'What would your mother say about your proposal?' Marie asked, not pursuing that line.

He sat back and stared at her from under his lashes.

'My mother will accept it. She will have no choice.' He paused. 'In fact, I don't see a great deal of her. Our relations are strained.' His mouth twisted bitterly and his expression was shuttered. That, it implied, was the end of the discussion.

'Think about it,' he said in a tone that expected no rebellion.

'I'll think about it.'

'And then think about Hattie.'

She didn't say anything, but his words played over and over in her head and the rest of the meal passed in a blur of confusion and unfocused anger.

Three hours later she was back home, and when, after dinner, Hattie was safely in bed asleep, she told her aunt about Holden's proposal. They were sitting in the lounge, with the television providing a low background murmur.

'He's managed to trap me,' Marie said helplessly. 'Get married for Hattie's sake. He knows my Achilles' heel.'

'Now I wonder why he would want to do that,' Edith remarked, surprised. 'I didn't think that illegitimacy in this day and age was something that forced young people into marriage.'

'You don't know him. He wants his daughter full-time and if this is the only way, then so be it. And anyway, he isn't young.'

Edith looked thoughtful. 'So when will this marriage take place?'

'As soon as the operation is over,' Marie said. 'The sooner the better, he told me. He thinks that I shall try and wriggle out of it if I can, so he's made sure that the handcuffs are open, but only just.'

'It will be for the best,' her aunt said slowly. 'She would benefit from having both parents supporting her.'

It sounded selfish, but Marie thought bitterly, and where do I fit in? Holden Greystone didn't give one damn about *her*. He never had. She had appealed to him physically, so he had used her and now he was using her again, to gain entry into his daughter's life.

Had he engineered that outing to the park so that he could prove his point? she wondered. Had he wanted to demonstrate how fulfilling for Hattie a family of three could be?

If so he had succeeded, because before the day was done she knew what her answer was going to be. Hardly what she had envisaged for herself all those years ago when she fell in love with him and dreams of being his wife had crept silently into her head, before reality had abruptly killed them off for good.

CHAPTER EIGHT

ANXIETY has a way of pushing everything into the background, but the thought of marrying Holden nagged away at her. It was like having five cracked ribs and a broken finger. The cracked ribs took precedence but you couldn't forget that the broken finger was still there and would hurt like hell once the ribs stopped paining.

There were all those desolate hours lying ahead of her and the only thing that could fill them was anxiety.

'Worry,' Holden had told her wryly the day before, as he dropped her off to Edith's house, 'is a futile emotion when nothing can be solved through it.'

'Is that what your computer brain has come up with for dealing with this situation?' she had asked with biting sarcasm, and he had frowned, his mouth tight.

'You can't let Hattie see how nervous you are. That will just make her nervous as well. She may only be a child, but she can still pick up vibes from you and react to them.'

Marie had glared at him, hating him just at that moment for having pointed out something which was perfectly obvious, and which she would have thought of on her own, thank you very much.

'Don't tell me how to run my life!' she had snapped.

He had ignored that. 'And,' he had continued without emphasis, 'don't forget that I shall expect your answer in the morning.'

Marie didn't think that she would be able to court sleep at all, but in fact she fell asleep early and slept soundly, and she didn't feel nervous at all, not really. Tense perhaps, but as she and Edith headed for the hospital, with Hattie sandwiched between them in the back of the taxi, she felt an enormous sense of relief.

Holden was waiting for them. He had already checked in and looked calm and casual and in control.

He looked at Hattie and then squatted down next to her and held her hand, engulfing it with his long fingers.

'Big day today, little one,' he murmured and Marie felt a lump of emotion in her throat. Hattie was getting that mesmerised look that she had had the day before.

'I'm not scared,' she said in her high, childish voice. 'I'm only scared of snakes and whales and spiders. There was a spider in Mummy's bath yesterday.'

Marie stroked her hair, which as always defied control, and wondered how courage could be so difficult to summon. Her aunt, next to her, was looking equally unsteady.

'Well,' Holden murmured in the same gentle, even voice, 'not too many of those around here, so you're quite right not to be scared. Nor am I, when you put it like that.'

He glanced up at Marie and as their eyes met she felt an odd twinge of emotion. Something stirred inside her, something familiar, which she didn't welcome and she looked away hurriedly.

The nurse was coming across, and the moment was lost as the wheels of hospital officialdom churned into action. The staff were brisk, sympathetic, and showed Hattie, herself and Edith to a room which was decorated with murals of nursery rhymes and full of children's books.

'It helps,' the nurse said, 'if children aren't faced with white, clinical room. All this—' she gestured around her

'—puts them at their ease and they don't contemplate
what lies ahead with the same degree of concern. Not,'
she added, 'that this little one will have the same level of
fear as an older child.'

Hattie was looking subdued and Marie squeezed her
hand tightly.

'We've got Mr Greystone in a room just along the corridor,' the nurse said conversationally, showing a profes-
sional lack of interest in their marital situation, and it was
only when her aunt said, after a long while, in a low
whisper, that perhaps she ought to see how Holden was
getting along, that Marie felt again that little jolt reminding her how much her life had been changed by his reappearance.

'I'll stay here with Hattie,' Edith murmured. 'You
mustn't forget that Holden is to be operated on as well. I
know you'd rather, but like it or not, he's Hattie's father
and soon will be your husband.'

'A marriage of convenience,' Marie said in the same
low voice. His convenience, she would have liked to add,
but then that would almost certainly have involved a
lengthy debate on the subject, and here was hardly the
time or the place.

Her aunt, she had realised, liked Holden and did not
disapprove of the hasty marriage. It was illogical, she had
told Marie the evening before, to think that because they
did not love one another the marriage would not be a
stable one. Love, she had said, was no guarantee of wed-
ded bliss. Many couples married with love in their eyes
only to find themselves hurling plates at each other one
year down the line. Which had not made her feel better
in the slightest.

She hovered in the hospital room for a while longer
loath to leave, holding Hattie's hand and trying to sound

normal and cheerful instead of on the brink of tears, while nurses entered and let on a seemingly never-ending cycle of temperature-taking, blood-pressure-taking and note-making. Then, catching her aunt's eye across the bed, she said on an impatient sigh, 'Oh, all right, all right. I'll go!'

She kissed Hattie, lingered some more and then wandered off in search of Holden's room, which she found with no problem. He was sitting indolently in the chair by the bed, smiling while a pretty nurse with red hair and freckles fussed over him.

The nurse straightened as Marie entered the room and the coy, flirtatious smile was replaced with the standard crisp bedside manner, which seemed to amuse Holden no end.

'You should be nervous,' she said accusingly, after she had shut the door behind her on his instructions. She perched on the side of the bed and looked at him. In the white hospital gown he looked bronzed and virile and through the gap at the front she could glimpse the muscular chest. No wonder that little red-haired nurse had been blushing and smiling, Marie thought drily, he didn't look like a patient, he looked like a sex symbol.

'Becky has been putting me at my ease,' he drawled, standing up and lounging against the windowsill, not taking any great pains to wrap the hospital gown around him.

'I'm sure,' Marie said calmly. 'I noticed, as a matter of fact.'

'And you disapprove? Why? Jealous?'

He watched her with lazy amusement in his grey eyes and she said sarcastically,

'Oh, yes, consumed with it.' Nothing could be further from the truth, her words implied, but then she thought with shock that yes, she had been jealous. She had seen him with that little nurse and had been hit with blind, irrational jealousy. The realisation knocked her sideways for a moment.

'How's Hattie?' he asked. 'I shall pop along and visit her in a little while, before they give her that injection to make her dozy, although I don't think that'll be for some time yet.'

'She seems OK,' Marie answered. There was a knock on the door and the nurse reappeared, eyes lowered even though the pink mouth was trembling on the brink of a smile.

'You've come back,' Holden murmured, his eyes warm with charm. He held out his arm while his blood-pressure was taken, and said in a deep, lingering voice, 'You'll have to every fifteen minutes, you know.'

'And why is that, Mr Greystone?' She had a soft Scottish accent and, even with her back to her, Marie could hear the smile in the words. She folded her arms and pursed her lips.

'To boost my courage levels, of course. I'm just a poor old patient, after all, quaking at the thought of going under the surgeon's knife.'

The nurse glanced up quickly and said in a voice that tried very hard to be detached, 'There's nothing to be afraid of. Mr Keriaki is an expert at these operations. You'll be in the best possible hands.'

'I think I am already,' Holden murmured and she giggled, before retreating with effort into her detached role, her head lowered as she entered his blood-pressure reading on the clipboard at the end of the bed.

'You're just a poor old patient, are you?' Marie said as soon as the nurse had left, 'quaking at the thought of being under the surgeon's knife?'

'She's rather pretty, don't you think?' Holden asked by way of response. 'All that red hair and freckles. I used to go out with a girl who looked a bit like that when I was in my teens.'

'Fascinating.'

He was, she realised, in a provocative mood. Maybe it was his way of dealing with what lay ahead. Everyone responded to the prospect of something daunting in different ways, she supposed.

'I thought you might say that.' He grinned and moved away from the window towards her, and instantly her body stiffened. Why did he have this effect on her? As soon as he got close to her, every nerve in her body seemed to jump to attention and she felt as though she were on fire.

Because, a little voice whispered gleefully, you're still in love with him. The blood drained away from her face and she looked at him with real alarm now.

In love with him? That was years ago, she told herself, but hard on the heels of that came a flurry of images and a thousand thoughts that left her head reeling.

Dry-mouthed, she knew that she had rationalised her reaction to him as a mixture of bitter, disillusioned dislike and stupid physical attraction. The physical attraction had panicked her at first, but then she had told herself that it wasn't unusual, after all, she had slept with him, and after all, he was an intensely attractive man.

Now she knew, with blinding clarity, that the pull she had felt was not just the uninvited face of desire rearing its head. She had quite simply never stopped loving Holden Greystone.

The realisation horrified her. He didn't love her. He had never loved her, and he never would. Here she was, back to square one, in love with a man whose indifference to her emotions would inevitably be the knife that would kill her, and worse, in a position from which there was no possible retreat. She could hardly run away as she had the last time because there was a child involved, not to mention the small matter of a forthcoming marriage.

'So,' he said, moving to stand in front of her, and she had to resist the urge to hastily step backwards, 'shall we dispense with the small talk? Are you going to marry me?'

'I can't think of anything I'd rather do less,' she muttered, meaning it, feeling only a sort of trapped, desperate dread at the prospect of being married to him, of having him physically within her reach but emotionally as distant as the moon.

His brows jerked together in a frown of displeasure, and she was heavily tempted to stick to that but then she thought of Hattie, she thought of the already growing trust she had shown in him, and the fulfilment she would undoubtedly get at being the centre of two adoring parents, and she continued, with reluctance, 'But I've decided to accept your proposal.' She looked at him with stubborn defiance. 'You gave me no other option, did you?'

'If I gave you what you wanted,' he grated harshly, 'you would have walked right back out of my life the minute this operation was over, taking my daughter with you.'

'Can you blame me?'

'Surely the prospect of marrying one of the most eligible bachelors in the country isn't that dire a thought,' Holden mocked. 'If I recall, your bet was to see who you could trap, and you've succeeded in winning the bet, even though your victory came a little late.'

'I hate you!' she flung at him, and he pulled her towards him. As her body hit his, she felt the drag of her senses and fought against it.

'Hate can be a passionate emotion,' he muttered. His mouth crushed hers with force, the impact throwing he head back, and she groaned with a mixture of desperation and desire as his lips found the curve of her neck and his hands moved to cup her breasts. She struggled, and she realised with horror that her struggle was mostly with herself, to resist the heady impulse flooding through her, telling her to return his kiss because that was what she wanted.

He released her abruptly and turned away, moving to stand by the window, and she remained where she was, trembling but unable to leave.

'You don't understand,' she said tightly, and he turned slowly to face her, his light eyes hooded.

'What don't I understand?'

'You're rich, yes, you're eligible, yes, but you've destroyed the fabric of my life.'

'Only in your fevered, over-imaginative mind,' he said negligently, which made her flush with anger. 'You also seem conveniently to forget that my life has been turned on its head as well.'

'Which is why,' she said with a last stab of hope, 'we can amicably sort this out without doing anything drastic.'

He shook his head. 'No. No visitation rights, no snacks in fast food bars at weekends. No man coming along to usurp my place in my daughter's life.'

She could have screamed.

'In that case, I have a few ground rules,' she said, stifling her anger and speaking very calmly, 'number one being no carrying on like you were doing a moment ago.'

'What are you talking about?'

'I'm talking about you! Flirting with that nurse. Oh, I don't care about that, but it's the prospect of a life full of your flirting, running round, making rules for yourself while you preach to me about that happy family life! How do you think I feel? I was happy until you came along.'

'I didn't come along.' His voice was like a whiplash. 'You showed up on my doorstep with a bomb in your hands. You must have been crazy if you thought that I'd go along with whatever you had in mind, let you sort out my destiny for me, decide where and when and how I got to see my daughter, without disturbing your damn life, of course. Grow up, Marie!'

There was a knock on the door and he said in a hard, rapid voice, 'Kiss me!'

'What?'

He pulled her towards him and she could feel her heart fluttering in her chest like a wild bird caught in a cage.

'Kiss me! You're my fiancée now and you'll damn well show it to the world.'

'I thought you didn't care what people thought,' Marie muttered desperately under her breath, and he shot her an odd, restless look.

The door opened and his mouth descended on hers, hard, hungry and coaxing a hungry response out of her without too much difficulty. Then he raised his face, looked over his shoulder and said with a grin, 'I keep telling my fiancée not to worry, that there will be more of those when this operation is over and done with.'

'Oh, yes, Miss Stephens,' the Scottish voice said from behind her, 'it'll be just fine. I must ask you to go now, though. We're about to administer the pre-med.'

'Wish me luck, darling,' Holden said huskily.

Marie looked at him uncertainly. There was tremendous sincerity and persuasion in his grey eyes and she wondered whether this was still all an act to impress the ward sister. She had never known him to try and impress anyone. She lowered her eyes and said huskily, 'Good luck.'

'How wonderful to have such a caring fiancée,' he murmured, pulling her towards him, his hand in her hair, and she looked at him sharply.

'Isn't it?' she murmured back.

'You'll be here when I next wake up.' He said that as a statement of fact, but there was a hesitant question behind it, and for the first time she realised that he really was nervous about the operation, however relaxed he appeared to be.

'I will,' she said, finding herself smiling, and his muscles relaxed. 'And good luck, Holden, from the bottom of my heart.'

'I must ask you to leave now, Miss Stephens,' the nurse said sympathetically from behind her, and when Marie stood up she could feel her heart beating heavily inside her. Proximity to Holden always did that to her, she acknowledged, and especially when her guard was down. The grey eyes held hers, and she could feel them on her as she walked towards the door, shutting it quietly behind her.

She had decided in advance that she would wait at the hospital until the operation was over, despite the doctor's assurances that she would be better off vanishing for a while to do some shopping, or else to have a cup of coffee somewhere, anything to preoccupy her mind, but Marie couldn't face the thought of not being physically in the same building as her daughter when this momentous event was taking place. It would have seemed treacherous.

She and her aunt went to the hospital canteen and the process of bolstering each other's morale proceeded in fits and starts, with anxious silences stretching between them, followed by outbursts of conversation about nothing in particular.

'Have you set a date for the wedding yet?' Edith asked

conversationally, and Marie had to gather her thoughts together to know what she was talking about.

'Not really,' she said, shifting her gaze away. 'At least, not that he's informed me, though knowing him he'll spring it on me when I'm least expecting it.'

'I shall miss you when you go, and of course Hattie when she comes out.' This time it was her aunt's turn to look away and there was a misty glimmer in her eyes. 'I've never said this, but you've both been a life-saver for me. I spent a life of bitterness and you ended that.'

'We shall come and see you whenever you want us to!' Marie said inadequately.

'He'll be good to you,' Edith said. 'He's quite different from what you told me about him, you know. He's a kind man.'

'Kind?' She thought of Holden in one of his jeering moments, his mouth twisted into an expression of mocking cruelty. 'Wrong person, Edith.'

Edith laughed and looked as though she were about to add something to her statement, but instead she changed the subject and they resumed their staccato, self-absorbed conversation, only breaking off to stretch their legs in the hospital car park.

It was difficult to believe that time could move quite so slowly. She had to force herself not to consult her watch every five minutes, because that depressed her, so that when her aunt touched her arm and told her that she thought they could start meandering towards the ward, Marie felt a start of dreadful anticipation followed swiftly by sheer terror. She held her aunt's arm for support and even that felt horribly inadequate.

When the surgeon finally emerged into the corridor she had a swooning sensation, and her mouth felt as though it had been frozen into immobility. She looked at the approaching figure, followed by his green-gowned assistants, and discovered that she couldn't actually say a word.

The chief surgeon was a tall, thin man with dark hair and the sort of intelligent, angular face that bordered on impatient. Marie suspected that he probably terrified the life out of his interns but inspired a great deal of confidence in his patients.

'Ah, Miss Stephens,' he said, while his assistants looked on with reverence.

'How did it go?' Edith asked, and Marie stared helplessly on because her mouth still felt full of cotton wool. She was trying to read the expression on the surgeon's face. Did he look hopeful or did that slight frown herald bad news? She had been reassured beforehand that everything would go all right, but there was no such thing as a foregone conclusion, was there? Even routine appendectomies could go horribly wrong, couldn't they? She hated thinking like that, but she couldn't seem to help herself.

'I am very satisfied indeed with the outcome,' he said in his calm, concise voice.

'Is my little baby going to be all right?' Marie croaked and he smiled.

'They both will. It was very successful. I don't foresee any problems.'

'When can we see them?' she asked, and she was told that she could see them straight away, but that she shouldn't expect a response. They were both resting.

He looked at his watch, informed her that he would be around to see them in a couple of hours' time and that she should feel free to ask any questions then.

Marie had carried around the weight of her daughter's illness for so long that it was impossible to shed it all in one go, despite the doctor's words. She went to see Hattie, who looked terribly frail, and she clutched her hand, wanting badly to let go of her worry. Gradually she began to draw sustenance from the unmoving figure. It was going to be all right. Doctors never uttered the word 'successful' unless an operation really had been. They almost always preferred to err on the side of caution.

'I'll just pop in and see Holden,' she told her aunt, who nodded, and now it struck her that underneath all that worry about Hattie there was a great deal about Holden himself.

She pushed open the door and her heart gave an unexpected jolt at the sight of him lying on the bed, eyes closed, his face robbed of its usual bronzed colour.

She went over to the bed and hesitantly held one hand.

'Thank you,' she whispered after a while. 'I know you probably can't hear me, but the doctor says that everything went just fine.' She paused, then murmured wickedly, safe in the knowledge that he was oblivious to her words, 'You look terrible. No colour at all.'

'Thank you.' His eyes opened and he stared at her, his mouth curved with wry amusement.

'You!' She went bright red. 'You should be sleeping.'

'I was, until you came in.' He smiled a little weakly at her. 'I would have said something sooner, but I couldn't resist being at the receiving end of some sympathy from you. It's so unusual.'

She tried to slip her hand out of his grip, but he held on to her, and in the end she gave up even though the warmth of his skin next to hers was making her feel very unsteady.

'How is Hattie?'

'Sleeping,' Marie said. 'She looks small and frail but she's going to be all right.'

He nodded and she asked awkwardly, 'How do you feel?'

'Probably exactly how I look.' His eyes narrowed on her with drowsy amusement. 'At this point, you're supposed to tell me that I look great.'

'You look great.'

'Little liar,' he murmured, with a smile. There was a warmth in his voice that reminded her of other days, years ago, when she had been fool enough to believe that he actually cared for her.

'All right then,' she said briskly, 'you look awfully pale. I don't think the little Scottish nurse would find you quite so appealing at the moment.'

'Oh, I don't know,' he murmured with weak amusement, 'some women find an ailing man quite irresistible.'

The way his eyes were roving over her made her feel uneasy, and she said hurriedly, 'I'm sure you could tell me all about that, but you really ought to be sleeping. The doctor would be very surprised to find you up and chatting.'

'Thank you for your concern, but as a matter of fact this operation is far easier on me than it is on Hattie. In a few days' time, I'll be back to my normal self.'

'Is that a good thing, I wonder?' Marie couldn't help asking, and he grinned.

All this relaxed charm, she thought, as though there had never been any ill feeling between them. He must still be under the effects of the anaesthetic. In a minute it'll wear off and he'll be at my throat.

'When you forget how much you hate me,' he murmured, 'you're far more like the girl I...used to know. This is why our marriage isn't doomed to failure as you assume it is. All you need to do is let down your guard.'

And be hurt by you again? she wondered. Her mouth

tightened into an obstinate line and she heard him sigh impatiently under his breath.

'There you go,' he muttered, 'closing up on me like a damned clam. I'm the one who should still be waging war. Has that occurred to you? Not that I feel up to waging anything right at the moment.'

Confusedly she thought that he had a point, though she wasn't about to admit that. She wasn't about to let her guard down, she wasn't about to let him see how much she still cared about him. Her heart skipped a beat, but now that she had admitted that much to herself, she couldn't retrace her steps.

How could I still be in love with him? she thought in desperation. She had never stopped loving him, she had just managed to persuade herself that she had. Three years ago she had told her stubborn mind that he was a bastard and she had continued repeating it over the years, like a refrain, so that after a while she had half begun to believe it. But seeing him again, hearing his voice, had been a sharp lesson in curing her of her self-delusion.

'No,' she agreed, thinking that he was below par and arguing with him was thoughtless and stupid, and besides, she didn't want to argue with him. 'You don't look as though you'd emerge the victor.'

'I hope that doesn't mean that you'll take advantage of me in my weakened state,' he said, looking at her from under his lashes, and she shook her head with resigned amusement.

'You never give up, do you?' she asked, but without hostility or any of the defences she had grown accustomed to erecting.

'Not when it comes to certain things,' Holden replied ambiguously. He smiled and gave her a glittering look.

'Anyway, feel free to take advantage of me in my weak-ened state.'

'I might,' she teased, ignoring his obvious meaning, 'but I can't think of anything I would want to take ad-vantage of you for.'

'Do you mean that?'

'Of course I do.' He was staring at her intently and she stood up abruptly, anxious to be out of the room.

'You really ought to rest now,' she told him, pulling her hand free.

'You mean so that you can run away?'

'No,' she answered more sharply than she had intended. 'You've just had an operation, there's no point in tiring yourself out unnecessarily,' she continued more gently.

She began moving towards the door and he said after her, 'I'll expect you tomorrow, shall I?'

She glanced over her shoulder but his expression was unreadable.

'If you feel up to it,' she said, which sounded utterly ridiculous even to her own ears, because he was up to it now, and tomorrow he would be feeling better, if any-thing.

'You mean if you do.'

There was no answer to that one and she turned on her heel and left the room quickly before her nerves went through the shredder completely and she ended up doing something silly like clutching him and pouring out her feelings.

It was a while later before she left the hospital with her aunt. She had spoken with the consultant, had asked all sorts of questions and had seen for herself, when Hattie had awakened, that it wouldn't be long before she was on the mend. She was already sounding cheery, though tired and letting it be known that she was hungry. For ice-cream, of all things. And also, where were her plasters? Her finger, which she stuck up and which was promptly kissed by Marie, *needed* one, and, Mummy, *you prom-ised*!

By the time she made it home, she felt exhausted. She and her aunt ate together, mostly in companionable si-lence, and then she made her way to bed where she fell rapidly asleep.

Over the next two days she and her aunt fell into a routine of going to the hospital, and, much as she hated to admit it, seeing Holden gave her a sharp thrill of an-ticipation.

Several of his staff had visited, along with some of his friends, and the room was laden with flowers and fruit, much of which remained uneaten. There had still been no visit from his mother, and when she asked him about that, he muttered uncomfortably that he had not told her about the operation.

'You mean she doesn't know about us? Or...or any-thing?' Marie exclaimed, horrified, and he shrugged sheepishly, not meeting her eyes.

'I shall have to phone her,' she said, dreading the pros-pect, and he remained silent.

'Let's sort ourselves out before you think of doing any-thing of the sort,' he muttered gruffly. He was wearing a silk robe, sitting in the chair by the window so that the light fell on his face, throwing it into disturbingly sexy angles. He had not been shaving, and the resultant stubble gave him a rakish, dangerous look, not that she needed any physical reminder that he was a threat.

'I leave tomorrow,' he said, and she nodded.

'Yes, I know. The nurse told me. Hattie will stay on for quite a while longer. Her blood has to be continually monitored, but everything's progressing nicely.' She smiled. 'I can't believe it's all over. I keep thinking that I should be worried, that it's somehow wrong to be so carefree and light-headed.'

'That's because you've spent so long with worry being your constant companion.' He paused and looked away. 'I suppose you'll want to give me a lift back to my apartment.' There was dull colour on his cheeks which made him appear boyish and unusually vulnerable.

'I suppose I will,' Marie mused, trying not to smile. 'I suppose I shall also want to cook you a meal, a way of saying thank you.'

'Of course.' He looked at her with some of his old arrogance back on his face, except that she knew him well enough now to see that there was something touching about the arrogance.

'But,' she warned, 'I'm no gourmet cook.'

'I'm very partial to sausages, mashed potatoes, beans and gravy,' he replied promptly.

'Are you really?'

'What a revelation!' he mocked in an incredulous voice, and she laughed.

Something had changed between them, and she didn't want to allow herself to believe that that meant anything. He was still full of bitterness towards her; it was there in the harsh lines of his mouth occasionally, and there was no point in deluding herself that he wasn't. Hattie was a bridge between them but any real understanding had to come from themselves and she couldn't see that happening. This, she told herself, was a temporary lull. An irresistible one.

He watched her until the door was firmly closed behind her but in fact she didn't immediately leave. She leaned against the closed door on unsteady legs and thought of the days and the nights that they would spend together as Mr and Mrs Greystone, and told herself that she couldn't afford to let him sweep her off her feet again.

CHAPTER NINE

HOLDEN was waiting for her the following day, after she had visited Hattie. She knocked on his door and then pushed it open to find him lounging against the windowsill and she immediately wanted to shut back the door and flee down the hospital corridor, back to the safety of her aunt's house.

With all the worry and upset over the past few days, the prospect of the final, inevitable forthcoming step looming in front of her had been shoved conveniently into the background, and it was only now, face to face with him, ready to leave the hospital, that she began to feel true, mounting apprehension.

She licked her lips nervously and wished that he wouldn't just stand there, staring, deliberately trying to make her feel uncomfortable.

They had not yet explained the situation to Hattie, but Holden had visited his daughter every day, building up a rapport between them, cementing the groundwork so that when she learned of his identity it would not come as an unpleasant shock.

'So,' she said, standing by the door, 'here I am. How are you feeling?'

'Never felt better,' he said, which made her mouth curve into a dry smile.

'Haven't you got to see the doctor, or the nurse or somebody before you go?' she asked, as he reached for his tan case, and he stopped to look up at her, his eyes impassive.

'All done. Temperature taken, blood-pressure taken, notes made, and I've passed the necessary MOT.' He paused and frowned, his grey eyes intent. 'You look like a terrified rabbit. Why? Do you dislike me that much?'

'Would you blame me if I did?' Marie asked, and his mouth tightened. It all came back to this, didn't it? she thought with a wave of despair. She couldn't let go of her sense of betrayal just as he could never let go of his sense of distrust.

'You're hardly a pillar of virtue,' he said coolly. 'At least,' he added, 'you were never the object of a wager.'

She opened her mouth to deny that, then she closed it again. His misconception was her safeguard, she thought. If he disliked her, then wasn't it only fair that he thought the feeling mutual?

'Shall we go?' she asked wearily, which made him frown even more.

'If you can bear it. What do you think I shall do now that I'm no longer safely confined to a hospital bed? Jump on you? Rape you?'

'Of course not,' Marie said uncomfortably. She could see from the set of his jaw that he was angry. He moved to where she was standing and looked down on her, his eyes flint-hard.

'Then why the hell don't you stop acting as though you're about to enter the lion's den?'

'How do you expect me to feel?' she asked. 'This isn't a normal situation, is it?'

'We're going to be married,' he said bluntly, his voice cold. 'How much more normal can you get? Don't you think that travelling to and fro to see Harriet, trying mathematically to work out the best times, would have been a far more abnormal situation?'

Marie didn't answer. He wasn't about to see her point of view, because he didn't want to. He had wanted his daughter on a full-time basis, and if marriage was the means to that end, then so be it. Since he didn't believe in love, why should it matter to him that there would be none?

He took her arm and she stiffened. She would never overcome this reaction to him, she thought with despair. She was desperately in love with him and every time he touched her, every time she was reminded how one-way the situation was, she would close up, a self-defence mechanism to limit the damage he could inflict on her.

'There you go again,' he muttered between his teeth. 'Sometimes I could hit you.'

'Oh, wonderful,' she replied in a jumpy voice. 'What an exciting prospect I have to look forward to. Living with a man who's tempted to hit me!'

'Oh, stop arguing, you witch,' he muttered, glancing at her and raking his fingers through his hair.

She opened her mouth to argue the point and he raised his eyebrows.

'I'm not a witch,' she confined herself to saying feebly, and he looked as though he didn't quite believe her.

'What's in the carrier bag?' he asked, changing the subject, and she shrugged.

'If you must know, a few potions and bits of bats' wing,' she said tartly, looking away because his remark had stung her, and not seeing the sudden twitch of his mouth. 'Actually, it's the ingredients for this meal I rashly promised to make you.'

'I'm hungry already. The food here has been less than wonderful.'

He propelled her out of the door, along the corridor, to the reception desk, where a handful of nurses were standing around, a couple of them reading notes, the rest chatting.

He approached them, and the tension which she had witnessed only seconds earlier had vanished. That dark, sexy face was smiling, charming, his voice teasing as he bantered with the women, and she felt a swift pang of bitter jealousy. She had to force herself to smile at them.

He continued to propel her along the corridor to the lift, but once they were inside his hand dropped to his side and they travelled the short distance down in silence.

He hates me, she thought miserably. Oh, he might want me physically, and he might joke with me occasionally, but deep down he'll always hate me for walking out on him, and for keeping Hattie a three-year secret.

They walked towards the car park and she silently let herself in, leaning across to unlock the passenger door.

He gave her directions to his apartment in a preoccupied voice, and she followed them in silence, preferring the company of her thoughts to the possibility of another argument with him.

When she pulled up outside the block of flats, he turned to her and said, 'Look, shall we call a truce? We have nothing to gain from taking swipes at one another, have we?'

'I guess not,' Marie said with a little sigh.

'Shake hands?'

She held out her hand and he linked his fingers through hers and she felt a dizzy sensation rush through her. There was an electricity between them that filled the car and made her head swim. She looked into his light, mesmerising eyes and said, 'Don't.'

'Don't what, Marie?' he asked softly.

'Don't...' Her mouth felt dry. 'Just don't.'

'Why not?'

'Because I couldn't bear it,' she blurted out truthfully. He wanted to kiss her, the intent was written in his silence, and she didn't think that she could stand the physical contact. It terrified her because she knew what would be released: love, passion, desire, all the things that she wanted to keep to herself, terrible secrets which she couldn't share with him without relinquishing her pride in the process.

He let her go and turned away. 'Very well,' he muttered, angry, 'but when you're my wife, you'll be my wife in more than name only.' He looked at her and his eyes were savage. 'You'll sleep with me and you'll make love with me, and dammit, you'll enjoy it.'

'Is that a command, Holden?' she asked, and he slung open the car door, turning to face her.

'It's a promise of things to come,' he grated.

They began walking towards the entrance of the building, and she stole a sidelong glance at him. He didn't look like a man who was just returning from hospital. He looked as powerful and vital as ever, and her heart skipped a beat at the thought that this man was going to be her husband, at what he had said. He pushed open the glass door and she brushed past him, her body touching his fleetingly, and she felt that familiar pleasurable pain at the brief contact.

'I hope you're not expecting too much of this meal,' she said lightly, to cover up her response and to break the silence between them. He was right. What was the point of arguing relentlessly with one another? She would, she thought, act like an adult, a woman in control instead of a dithering adolescent.

'I don't cook well in other people's kitchens,' she continued, when her contribution to small talk met with no response.

'I know you want me,' he said, ignoring the remark and focusing his glittering eyes on her as they moved towards the lift.

The doors opened and they stepped inside. Marie didn't look at him. She looked at the panel on the side of the lift, she looked at the Open Door sign and the Close Door sign, she looked at the numbers of the floors, and she tried not to be completely overcome by the hammering going on inside her.

'Answer me!' He pulled her around to face him and she shrank back at the dark intensity of his gaze.

'I don't want to talk about this,' she said desperately.

'Why not?'

'Because there's no point!'

The lift stopped and the doors opened with a little ping, then shut back behind them.

'When we're married, I won't have you playing the shrinking violet on me,' he said savagely, opening the door to the apartment, slamming it behind her when they were inside.

'All we do is argue,' she said miserably. 'What's the point in us getting married if the best we can manage is to shout at one another?'

'You do something to me,' he muttered, and whatever it was she did to him, she thought, it wasn't good because his face was dark, brooding. 'I've always been in control of everything,' he said, 'but the minute I get near you—'

'You needn't spell it out,' Marie cut in stiffly, 'I get the message.'

She walked across to the small table and plopped the carrier bag down. His apartment was as she remembered, large, masculine, clinical.

'We can't argue all the time,' she said quietly, facing him, with her arms folded. 'It would be a terrible atmosphere for Hattie.'

'Yes,' he agreed coolly. He headed towards the kitchen and she followed in his wake.

The kitchen matched the rest of the apartment. Everything gleamed with a mixture of black and chrome, highly polished and full of all the latest gadgets. She stared at it and said truthfully, 'It looks unused. Do you ever use it?'

'Of course it's used,' he said, moving towards the fridge and offering her a drink of fresh juice, which she accepted. 'My manservant is very good when it comes to the culinary arts.'

There were three leather-topped stools by the counter and she sat on one, sipping the juice.

'Manservant?' Her face was astonished. 'You have someone who cooks for you?'

'As well as cleans the apartment and makes sure that everything is ticking over. Hattie will love him. He has ten grandchildren and is fond of expounding on the joys of those little pattering feet.'

It hardly surprised her when she stopped to think about it. Still, it was odd to think that, while she had struggled financially to bring up their child, less than one hour's drive away the man responsible for Hattie had been swanning into his personally tended apartment, complete with home-cooked gourmet meals. It was something that she had no intention of pointing out, however, not even as a joke, because she knew that his reaction would not be one of shared amusement.

'And is he responsible for this orange juice?' she asked, quite happy to keep the conversation on this fairly innocuous level.

Holden nodded. 'Came in every day and made sure that the fridge was well stocked for my return.'

'Very thoughtful.'

'He's paid to be.'

'I suppose he could have whipped up a delicious lunch for you today as well,' she pointed out, and the firm line of his mouth relaxed into a smile.

'I suppose he could have, but I rather like the thought of eating something prepared by your own fair hands. Besides, he's a trained chef, apart from anything else. I really only ask him to cook for me when I'm entertaining clients at home. If I want something simpler, I normally grab a takeaway or else do it myself.'

He walked to where she was still sitting on the stool, and said, without undertone, 'Better?'

He was close enough to disconcert, and her eyes widened in puzzlement.

'Better? What do you mean?'

'Polite conversation, no arguing—' his eyes stripped her very quickly, then returned to her face '—no touching.'

Marie went bright red and stammered, 'It's not pleasant to argue.' Which was a ridiculous remark but she couldn't think of a thing else to say.

'Now,' he said briskly, 'I'm going to have a bath. If you want to start cooking, everything in here is fairly self-explanatory...'

'Are you sure?' She eyed the kitchen dubiously. 'I feel as though I need a degree in computing to get to grips with all this.'

He grinned wryly, looking down at her with an amusement that made her head swim. She had told him that she didn't want to argue with him, that an atmosphere of constant bickering was worse for Hattie than the stability of two parents who just happened to live apart, but in truth she felt safe when she was arguing. She was on sure ground then. She slipped off the stool, neatly brushing past him, and peered at the oven, the grill, the stove, all gleaming as if they had just been carted in from a store.

'I'm sure I'll manage,' she told him, turning around to find him looking at her. 'If I don't burn the place down in the process.'

He laughed and said, 'I quite like char-grilled sausages.' Then he left the kitchen, headed off towards the bathroom, and she went into the lounge area to rescue the carrier bag.

First she set the table in the kitchen. It was a circular black table, very modern-looking, not to her taste at all, but attractive enough in its setting. She had to scout around a few cupboards, but in the end she found plates, glasses, cutlery, all very heavy and expensive and nothing like the sort of mismatched crockery which she had become accustomed to using at her aunt's house.

Then she began cooking, sticking the sausages under the grill, peeling the potatoes and putting them to boil, preparing the beans in a spicy barbecue sauce.

She found that she was rather enjoying herself. There were no worries about Hattie, and for the moment it was easy not to think about Holden and marriage and whatever problems that would entail.

She began making the gravy, humming under her breath, and she wasn't aware of Holden entering the kitchen until he spoke from just above her shoulder.

'Smells delicious,' he said, and she didn't look around.

'You're not supposed to see what I'm doing,' she informed him. 'It spoils the surprise.'

'It's not a surprise,' he pointed out. But he moved away nevertheless and returned a few minutes later with a glass of chilled white wine, which he placed on the kitchen counter.

'Cooks always drink as they work,' he said, half leaning on his elbow on the counter so that he could look at her.

Marie glanced sideways at him. He had changed into a short-sleeved faded blue shirt and a pair of jeans. She suddenly felt in dire need of a drink, and she gulped down some of the wine, which steadied her considerably.

'Did you keep in touch with any of the members of the crew on the liner?' he asked curiously, and Marie looked at him with some surprise.

'What makes you ask that?'

He shrugged and went to sit on one of the bar stools, which was better because he was no longer in her range of vision, with her back to him.

'I guess,' he said slowly, 'because you've changed quite a bit. Oh, I've seen glimpses of the girl I used to know, but you're different somehow. Much more self-confident.'

'You mean I look ten years older,' she said lightly, bending to chop the onions and tomatoes for the gravy.

'You know that's not what I mean at all.'

'Well, in answer to your question, no, I lost touch with them all. Jessica calls occasionally, but I preferred...'

'To put that part of your life behind you and pretend that it never existed?'

'Something like that,' she agreed, wiping her hands on the apron and frying the ingredients for the gravy. She wasn't looking at him; she couldn't read the expression on his face.

He didn't say anything. He poured her another glass of wine, then returned to the stool. She could feel his eyes on her back, watching her, and it made her uncomfortable.

It was a relief to begin setting the food on to platters, putting it all on the table, because it was a welcome distraction from his questions.

They sat down and she blushed as he made complimentary noises about the food. If his manservant preferred cooking gourmet delights, then she had mastered the art of the simple meal, and she watched with hidden pleasure as he helped himself to more, not forgetting to top up her glass.

She should, she knew, refuse the wine. Drinking at lunchtime was something she never did, and even with food in her stomach she could feel it going to her head. It made her very relaxed, and she wasn't quite sure if she wanted to be very relaxed.

For a while they talked about Hattie. She would be in the hospital for quite a while longer, because, the consultant had explained when she had looked worriedly at him, they wanted to make sure that she was exposed to no infections while she was recovering. They also wanted to make sure that she continued to respond well to the transplant, which meant regular blood tests.

'And you can stop frowning,' Holden said lazily, 'that's perfectly routine after a major operation like that.'

Normally she would have been tempted to launch into a self-defensive argument on the point, but instead she smiled at him, took another sip of wine, and thought in a pleasantly muddled way that he was very reassuring. It was nice sharing her concerns with him. In a strange way she trusted what he said and was comforted by it.

'Why,' she heard herself ask, 'have you never married, Holden?'

It seemed a logical question and she looked at him expectantly while he gave the matter some thought. For a moment, she didn't think that he would answer, and instead of pulling back in horror at what she had said she raised her eyebrows and looked at him challengingly.

'You want the story of my life?' he drawled, and she nodded. 'In that case, I think we ought to adjourn to the lounge. It's infinitely more comfortable for life stories.'

He stood up, and when she rose to follow him she felt a little wobbly, but nicely so. They went into the lounge and she sat next to him on the sofa, with the sun streaming in from behind, filling the room with bright, warm colour. It made the furnishings appear less harsh, more appealing.

'Life story, please,' she murmured, leaning back and looking at him from under her lashes, and he stared back at her with amusement.

'I think you've probably had too much to drink,' he said, and she shook her head in denial.

'Three glasses. Not much at all.'

'Well, the short answer to your question is that I've never been tempted. My parents are divorced, and divorce is something that rubs off on you. I'm not sure that you're in a sober enough state to take this in,' he murmured, flicking his eyes over her face, and she raised her hands behind her head, a sensual, graceful movement which she wasn't even aware of.

'I never talk about my past with anyone,' he said.

'Secretive. I know.'

He laughed. 'I like you like this.' There was a warm gleam in his eyes and her breathing quickened.

'You're trying to change the subject.'

'Is that what I'm doing?'

'It is. Changing the subject. I can read you like a book.'

'Can you indeed?' he said softly.

'So tell me.'

'All right. How's this for starters? I never respected my father.' He paused and there was a certain hesitancy in his silence. 'He was a weak man. He could never resist a pretty face and he was an inveterate spender. I realised that from early on. I can remember my mother telling me that he could be very charming, very polished, and that when they were first married she adored him for those characteristics, the very ones that would eventually doom their marriage to failure. He spent money like water. When I was ten years old he walked out on us, and it was only in the wake of his desertion that my mother, and then I, discovered the true cost of his treachery. He had gambled away all of the family money. Business deals that didn't pan out, pie-in-the-sky schemes that anyone with an ounce of common sense would have steered clear of. I had to be withdrawn from private school, which didn't bother me unduly, but upset my mother a great deal.'

'Yes,' Marie said soberly, 'it would. A loss in social standing can be very humiliating, I should imagine.'

'I worked like the devil to get to university.' His face had hardened. 'I built back the empire my father had squandered brick by bitter brick. Around me my friends were settling down, beginning to raise families, letting go their ambition in favour of family time. It wasn't for me. Marriage, I felt, was transitory. What lasted was etched in sweat and hard work. You could rely on your work far more than you could ever rely on another human being.'

Marie looked at him with some understanding. What he had told her explained a good deal. A person's present was often the product of their past. Holden had learnt power and cynicism at an early age and it had moulded him into the person he was today. Hard, ruthless, determined.

His expression was shuttered when he looked at her and

she realised that he was making sure that she didn't express pity.

'I hope I haven't bored you to tears,' he said roughly, and she shook her head.

'Not at all,' she murmured, when she really meant, you could never do that.

He stood up abruptly and informed her that he was going to wash the dishes.

'There's a dishwasher lurking around in the kitchen somewhere, but God help me if I have the faintest idea how to use it.'

'I'll help,' Marie told him, and they began clearing the table. She wondered whether he regretted his earlier confidences. There was a certain tautness in his body, even though his manner was easy enough.

She slipped on the apron and they worked efficiently together, ploughing through the dishes until everywhere was clear, and she squeezed the sponge with satisfaction.

'I'm far better than a dishwasher,' she teased, but when she raised her eyes to his there was no answering smile there. He looked intently at her and muttered, 'Damned sight sexier.'

She began fiddling behind her, trying to untie the apron, and he stepped forward and said, 'Let me do that for you.'

His arms wound around her and their bodies touched. It was as though a match had been set to dry tinder. Every pore in her body went up in flames and a gasp escaped her.

He wasn't talking, but she could feel the answering need in him and it flew to her head like incense. Was it the wine or was it what seemed like a lifetime of starvation that made her wrap her arms around him? She didn't know any longer, she only knew that she couldn't bear not to touch him.

'I want you,' she said on a sigh.

He had known that all along. They both had. What was the point in denying it?

She arched up to meet him, her mouth covering his, and he lifted her off her feet, carrying her towards the bedroom.

He pulled the curtains together and the midday light was immediately shut out. It had always seemed to her faintly decadent to be in a bedroom in the middle of the day, when the sun was shining, with the curtains closed. Right now she felt very decadent, absolutely wanton, and too light-headed to start questioning what she knew was about to take place between them.

She lay on the bed, and when he had joined her, she began unbuttoning her blouse, her fingers shaking.

'I've wanted you for so damned long,' he groaned, brushing aside her fingers feverishly to pull open her blouse. 'Ever since you walked into my office, I've done nothing but think about you.'

She moaned with pleasure as his mouth sought and found one hard nipple. She looked at his dark head sucking against her breast and then closed her eyes as a wave of intense pleasure ripped through her. When he stood up to remove his clothes, she watched him with abandonment, desire flaring in her eyes, and he gave her a slow smile.

'Do you like what you see, my darling?'

She laughed, her eyes half closed. 'Now will you do the same for me?'

'Is that the wine talking, I wonder?'

She didn't answer, but there was invitation in her eyes, and he lay down beside her, unzipped her skirt, which joined his discarded clothes on the ground, and eased his hand beneath her underwear.

She pulled him fiercely towards her and their mouths met with burning passion.

'I've wanted to ask, Marie,' he muttered against her, 'has there been anyone else?'

'No one,' she said, and he groaned as though her celibacy had fired some deeply buried response.

'Good.' He caressed her most intimate region, his fingers expertly exploring every inch of her, then with the palm of his hand he rubbed her to heady arousal.

She moved against him, groaning, and he said softly, 'Not yet.' He knelt to pull her lacy briefs down, then parted her legs, his mouth and tongue replacing his exploring fingers, sending her spinning into a world where thought ceased to exist.

When she felt that she could no longer bear it, he moved back to tease her nipple with his tongue, massaging both breasts with his hands, then she lazily eased her body over his and kissed his chest, her tongue darting over his torso, down to his hard, muscled stomach, to his arousal as urgent as her own was.

She sat over him, her body slim and supple, and lowered herself on to him, moving slowly at first, then with quickening urgency, his hands on her waist, his rhythm as smooth as hers, until they reached a pinnacle of pleasure and he gave a deep groan of release.

'Has it been three years, longer, since we last made love, Marie?' he asked drowsily. 'Before I touched you, it seemed like forever, but now it seems like yesterday.'

The euphoria brought about by the wine and her passion was dissolving fast. She looked at his hard-boned aggressive face with sinking dismay.

'I've wanted to make love with you ever since I first saw you again,' he said.

'And now you have.'

Holden Greystone, she was thinking, would never love, he never could, it was an ability which had been eradicated in his youth. He was, however, a strikingly attractive man with a great deal of sexual appeal, and if he couldn't love, he could desire. He had wanted her three years ago, and she had mistaken that want for a reflection of her own blind love. He still wanted her now and she knew that she should play the game along his rules, sleep with him, never mention love, but the prospect of a lifetime of that filled her with a certain amount of horror.

'And now I have,' he agreed with satisfaction.

'It's awful,' she said in a whisper, and he stiffened next to her. 'I just can't marry you,' she said brokenly. 'I would do anything for Hattie, anything, but not this.'

His body went rigid.

'What are you talking about?'

'I know that she would benefit from a family, but I just can't marry you,' Marie told him weakly, sitting up. 'I'm attracted to you, I won't bother to deny it, but our marriage would be empty, and however much we tried, we'd end up arguing, hating one another.'

'You don't know what you're talking about.'

He watched her, his eyes sharp and glittering.

'I just couldn't face it, Holden.'

'You don't know what you're talking about,' he repeated and there was savagery in his voice.

He sat up and looked at her and she whispered, 'How could you marry someone you hate?'

'I don't hate you,' he answered bluntly. 'All right, I admit that I did…then. What do you expect? I hear you talking about rich men on the liner as prospective catches, you tell me that you won me in a bet—what the hell did you expect? A ten-foot grin and a pat on the head?' He stared at her, and in the darkened room his eyes felt as though they were burning into her skin. 'I spent three years cursing you, and when you walked back into my office to ask a favour I wasn't in a forgiving mood. But I don't hate you. My first instincts about you were right. Use your head, girl! If you were a gold-digger, you would have come running to me the minute you found out you were pregnant. You would have demanded a ring on your finger and legitimacy for our child, and, much as I hated the fact that you didn't tell me about Hattie, it proved that you weren't what I thought you were.'

'All right then, you don't hate me.' But you don't love me either, do you? she asked herself silently, bitterly. 'And you were wrong about what you overheard. I was talking to Jessica, and yes she was carrying on about rich men, but it was a joke, and anyway I was hardly listening. Neither of us would ever have seen any of the men on that liner as prospective catches, as you put it.' She thought back to those carefree, sunny days, the easy rapport between them all. It seemed like decades ago. 'All the crew members used to speculate about the passengers, but only to pass the time. I was never interested in you for your money. I would never even have known about it if you hadn't told me!'

There was a revelation waiting on the air, but he didn't seize it. He said, 'Then what's the problem, for God's sake?' He gripped her shoulders and shook her slightly 'Wake up, Marie! I'm not a man accustomed to speak about my emotions, but I have, and you've admitted yourself that you want me.' His voice was thick, hoarse. 'And I want you! So what the hell is the problem?'

'I won't marry you.' She turned away.

'It's for Hattie,' he said urgently, and she shook her head.

'It would be sterile.'

There was a deafening silence, then he roared, making her jump, 'All right, then! Fine!' He stood up and began slipping on his clothes, not looking at her. She watched him with misery, wanting to touch him, to tell him that she would marry him after all, but knowing, as she had always known deep down, that without love their marriage would be nothing and, much as he desired her, it just wasn't enough.

'It wouldn't work,' she half pleaded, and he gave her a freezing look.

'You've said enough. I'm leaving. My lawyer will sort out visiting rights.'

He walked out of the room, and then, seconds later, she heard the slam of the front door, then she collapsed back on to the bed and began to cry. For the first time.

CHAPTER TEN

HATTIE was sitting on the bed, drawing. It was a picture of the family which comprised Edith and Marie and herself. Marie sat and watched and expressed delight with the stick figures with their large round heads and peculiar figures. She had already drawn four and was stacking them into a neat pile which she generously told her mother she could take away with her.

'I did one for Nurse Jenny,' she said, concentrating hard on what she was doing. 'She's going to put it on her wall.'

Marie looked at the diminutive figure with a sharp pang of love and regret that the family life which had hovered tantalisingly for a while had now vanished without trace.

'I think I need another plaster, Mummy,' Hattie said, looking up. 'On my arm. See? There.' She pointed to a freckle.

'It seems all right to me,' Marie said soothingly.

They had been sitting like this, contentedly chatting for the past half-hour, while Marie churned over in her mind every little detail of her bitter parting with Holden. She knew that it was pointless going over what she should and should not have done, but she couldn't seem to help it. Her mind had a will of its own and took a perverse pleasure in pointing out what a fool she had been. She had been so sure that she had immunized herself against him, that the passing of years had done their work, and now she despaired of ever really recovering. The very worst thing was that years ago her love had been a heady, reckless one, but this time it was stronger because little by little a deep friendship between them seemed to have developed somewhere along the way.

Hattie had now moved on from the subject of her arm and was transferring her concern to the My Little Pony, which she hopefully intimated also needed a plaster because she had fallen and Nurse Jenny had agreed that there might be a bruise. She held the pony up for inspection.

'All right,' Marie said, giving in, 'I'll try and remember to bring one next time.'

Hattie smiled and returned to the drawing, including a few animals in the scene, unidentifiable shapes which she patiently identified as a cow, a pig and a hen.

Marie appropriately said that she could recognise each one immediately, which was rewarded with a beam, and relapsed into her thoughts, hardly hearing the door open behind her. She didn't look around immediately, expecting it to be one of the nurses, but it wasn't. Holden's deep voice shocked her into rigidity, and she slowly turned to face him.

Hattie had dropped the pencil and was staring at him with wide, delighted eyes. Marie watched the scene from under lowered lashes. He had brought a parcel with him and he handed it to Hattie, who could hardly contain her excitement. It was a puzzle, a small twelve-piece one of a farm scene, with which she was engagingly pleased. The lump in Marie's throat grew a little larger, even though Holden had barely glanced in her direction and was focusing all his attention on his daughter.

'Pictures,' he said. 'May I have a look?'

Hattie handed him the little pile and he sifted through them and declared himself impressed.

'Can you see the animals?' she asked, and Marie said helpfully,

'I bet you can't recognise that they're a pig, a cow and a hen.'

For the first time he looked at her, his grey eyes unreadable.

'But of course!' he exclaimed, turning back to Hattie, who was giving an excellent imitation of a preening peacock.

She lay back on the pillows and closed her eyes. She was not going to be jumping about and full of beans, not just yet, the consultant had told Marie, but she was steadily progressing and would be home perhaps sooner than they had anticipated.

'Would you read me that story?' she asked Holden, and he looked down with some adoration on her.

'I know another one,' he said, and Hattie smiled with pleasure. 'It's about a little boy who lived in a big house. Shall I read that one to you?' Hattie yawned, and nodded, and he began telling a tale of a big house, a big pond, a small boy and a duck, making up as he went along, until Hattie's breathing became slow and rhythmic.

Holden continued, still not looking at Marie, his voice low and hypnotic.

'And then one day,' he said to his soundly sleeping daughter, 'the little boy, who was now a man, realised that he didn't know how to love.'

Marie shot him a sharp look.

'I don't think she can hear you,' she said, in as near normal a voice as she could muster.

'I should like to finish the story anyway,' he murmured. 'Outside. I think you might be interested in hearing it and if you aren't...' He was looking at her intently. 'There's a café on the first floor.'

They stood up, and Marie walked along with him to the café in bewildered silence. What story could he possibly want to continue and why might she be interested in it? Twice he had succeeded in ruining her life, so what more did he intend to do?

She waited until they were sitting down, then she said, taking the bull by the horns, 'Well? What did you want to talk to me about?'

Holden sipped from the cup of coffee. 'I have a story to finish,' he said quietly. 'A story about a man who thought he knew it all.'

'This man is you?'

'Who else?'

'I don't want to hear,' Marie said. She wanted to shut down all her systems, and listening to anything Holden had to say wasn't going to help her cause.

'When we first met,' he said heavily, disregarding her interruption, 'I felt as though I'd been hit on the head by something very large. You were so different from the women that I was accustomed to.'

Marie took a sip of coffee. Her feet were nailed to the floor and her heart was beating so loudly that she thought she could hear it. I'm not interested, she told herself, I'm only sitting here out of common politeness.

'To start with, I found that amusing. I felt like someone who has spent his life on a diet of rich food, only to be faced with something altogether simpler, only to find that his taste for that something is far greater than it ever was for the rich food. Do you understand what I'm saying?'

She managed a nod, even though the muscles in her neck were feeling as stiff as her legs. Yes, she understood, sort of, and foolishly her heart began to beat quicker.

'I left my apartment just now because I had to think.' He sighed and looked at her with uncustomary hesitancy.

'Lean forward,' he muttered, 'closer to me. I want to breathe you in while I talk.'

Marie leaned forward, which was just as well, she thought, because she would be able to hear him better over the steady, deafening roar in her ears.

When he had begun talking, this was not what she had expected. It was like opening a closed door, expecting to find a cupboard only to be confronted with an unexpected, breathtaking view of open countryside.

'I never expected you to get under my skin the way you did,' he said, and there was an accusing look in his eyes. 'I kept thinking of you day and night. I postponed my departure from the liner, even though there was work waiting for me back in London. My mother noticed and she began lecturing to me on your unsuitability.'

'Yes,' Marie nodded, travelling back in time, 'I received several lectures myself.'

'Poor you. My mother can be ferocious when the mood takes her. You should have said something to me.'

'Never! I thought that I could handle it.' Except, she mused to herself, I couldn't, could I? Mrs Greystone had struck where it had hurt most. She had held Marie up for examination, and had then discarded her on the basis of background. She had seized on the most vulnerable spot and Marie had been hurting ever since.

'Before I met you, I found my mother's interference in my private life a little irritating sometimes, a little amusing sometimes. I knew that she did it because she was protective. Occasionally I would humour her by taking out one of the girls from her stable of possibilities.' He laughed. 'They were always the same. Pretty, well-mannered, very enthusiastic about doing charity work because Daddy would always be there to provide for them.

Not a brain between them. Tiring to have around after a few hours.'

'A fate worse than death,' Marie said with a straight face, and he gave her a crooked smile. He reached out and idly stroked her arm with his finger.

'Then I met you. I wanted you the minute I saw you, do you know that? You became a drug, and this time when my mother decided to interfere I wasn't at all amused or irritated. I was furious, but she kept on and on and on.'

Marie nodded encouragingly. Her pulses were racing and she didn't want them to stop.

'I told her that I had no intention of paying a blind bit of notice to anything she had to say about you.'

'What?' Marie said sharply. The colour drained from her face and she was hurled back in time to the liner, to the cabin, to where she was standing by a half-open door, listening to a conversation that was making her sick.

'What's the matter?' He frowned and leaned forward, holding her arms.

'I've been a fool,' she muttered, putting her hand to her forehead. 'I thought...'

'What did you think? I'm not following you.'

'When did you have this conversation?' she asked weakly. 'I don't suppose you remember, it was a long time ago.'

'I remember exactly,' Holden said, 'because it was the day before I overheard that conversation between you and your friend, the day you told me that you'd been stringing me along for a bet and I felt so bloody murderous that I could have killed you. I thought I knew you, you see, and I had been wrong.'

There was a little silence while Marie gathered her addled wits together.

'I spent three years trying to get you out of my system,' he said in such a low voice that she had to strain forward to hear. 'And along the way had the most godawful argument with my mother who couldn't understand why I was so filthy mad when as far as she was concerned you and I were finished. She resumed her matchmaking with even more zeal until I told her in no uncertain terms that you were still on my mind and no amount of simpering young blondes was going to get you out of my system. I never told her that I'd discovered that you were only after my money. I couldn't stand the triumph she'd feel, and, more importantly, I just couldn't bring myself to say it. I hated you for having pulled the wool over my eyes, and I hated myself even more for not being able to rid myself of thoughts of you when I knew I should.'

'You couldn't?'

He shot her a rueful smile. 'Pathetic, wouldn't you say? You damn well sent me to hell, and that's something I never thought I'd say. I must be losing my mind.'

'I didn't think that we were suited,' Marie said, lowering her eyes. 'I didn't want to be hurt. I was in love with you.' She looked at him and said quickly, 'No, that's not all.' What would he think of her, she wondered, if he knew that she had eavesdropped on a conversation? 'I overheard you talking with your mother,' she said weakly. 'I got the impression that you were playing with me, using me, that you had no intention of it ever developing into anything more serious than a fling. That night, you see, I came looking for you—' still floating somewhere on cloud nine, she thought, still harbouring fairy-tale thoughts '—and you were arguing with your mother. About me. I shouldn't have stayed, but I did. Enough to hear some of what was being said before the door was closed, and…'

'And what you didn't hear, you filled in all by yourself.' His voice was terse.

'What can you expect?' Marie defended in a low, hot voice. 'You were rich, eligible, good-looking, and I'd been warned off you by your mother. Of course I thought that you would drop me the minute the novelty wore off! I was startled when you surprised me in the cabin with Jessica, and when you accused me of gold-digging, well, that really hurt, but I was already hurting and I was angry and confused, and I said the first thing that came into my head. I wanted to hurt you just as you had hurt me.'

'You should have explained,' he muttered.

'You weren't open to explanations. I saw that in a flash, and I realised, equally quickly, that you had probably expected me to live down to your expectations anyway. I didn't want to end up on the scrap heap, along with who knows how many other women!'

She looked at him mutinously, then he smiled at her, a slow smile that made her bones feel like water. 'You foolish girl,' he said huskily. 'You foolish girl.'

'You didn't love me!'

'I fell in love with you the minute I saw you.'

'What?' Was she sitting in a hospital café with metal chairs and gloomy paint on the walls? She felt as though she were soaring in some exquisitely beautiful place, far above everything and everyone.

'I love you,' he muttered. 'Satisfied?'

Satisfied? Would a starving beggar be satisfied if he unexpectedly scooped a million pounds on the football pools? Her eyes were luminous.

'When you walked into my office that morning, I couldn't believe it. For three years I'd kidded myself that you were where you belonged: out of my life. I'd gone out with other women, meaningless little affairs that meant nothing. The woman I'd been seeing when you stepped back into my life was beautiful, but I hadn't even touched her. Can you believe that?' He looked as though he hardly believed it himself. 'It had been a four-month relationship which was already going stale. You walked through that damned office door and I felt as though I'd suddenly awakened from a long dream, and I hated it.'

'I know,' she said reflectively. 'It was written on your face. Have you any idea how much courage I had to summon up to tell you about Hattie?'

'She brought us together,' Holden murmured. 'This,' he added, looking around, 'is not the best of places in which to have this conversation.'

'It'll do. I don't want to stop talking in case this is all a dream.'

'No dream, my darling.' He slanted a smile at her.

'What made you come here this afternoon?' Marie asked curiously.

'Fate?' He laughed shortly. 'When you told me that you weren't going to marry me, I felt as though I were going mad.' He lowered his eyes. 'I can't believe I'm saying all this. I've never been a man to talk about…this type of thing.' He shook his head with some wonder, then continued, 'I'd never thought of myself as the marrying kind, but I knew that I had to marry you, and I knew that I had to tell you that I loved you.'

'It was what I wanted to hear.'

'It took me a long time.' He paused. 'Something told me that you'd be at the hospital. I only hoped that it wasn't too late.'

'I love you, Holden Greystone! I never stopped. When I saw you again after all that time, it was as if I were back to square one.'

'Good,' he murmured. 'Because that's how I felt as

well. You stood there, looking as though you couldn't stand the sight of me, acting as though I was an unpleasant stranger, and all I could think was that you were the most beautiful thing that had ever come into my life. You'd caught me on a hook, and I hated myself for it.'

Under the narrow table their legs touched, and she knew that what she felt was a reflection of what he was feeling. This really wasn't the best place for this. She could think of somewhere far better.

'I knew,' he continued slowly, 'the minute you walked into my office, after three years of silence, that you wanted something from me and that gave me a kick. I thought what you were after was some money and the devil in me saw a thousand ways of making you pay the price for it. When you told me about Hattie, I saw red.'

'You don't have to remind me,' she said with a catch in her throat.

'Only later did I realise that Hattie gave you back to me, because I still wanted you, still loved you, much to my disgust, and I was determined to have you, you and our daughter.'

'You should have said,' she murmured.

'And risk watching your disbelief, not to mention your laughter?'

'I wouldn't have laughed.'

'How was I to know?'

'You could have trusted me.'

She looked at him from under her lashes and half smiled. 'Thank God everything went all right with Hattie,' she said on a wrenched sigh. 'I keep stopping and telling myself that she's OK now, that I don't have to live each day with a knot in my heart.'

'I guess, in a way, she brought us together,' Holden

said. 'Just as silly misunderstanding and suspicion drove
us apart.'

One of the women who had served them from behind
the counter came across with a battered tray, and eyed
them suspiciously.

'More coffee?' she asked in a voice that implied, if not,
then time to leave.

'We were just about to go,' Holden told her, and she
clattered away with their cups.

'Go where?'

'To Hattie's ward,' he said, as if that should have been
obvious. 'I think we should finish our discussion there,
and when Hattie wakes up we should go and tell her what
lies in store for her as soon as she comes out of hospital.'

'And what's that?' Marie asked teasingly, as they left
the café and sauntered towards the children's ward. It
would probably be empty. They would be surrounded by
toys and possibly be interrupted by occasional childish
chatter but, thinking about it, where better to be than close
to their daughter?

'A mother, a father.' He had his arm around her and
he bent to kiss her neck, a fleeting little kiss that felt
exquisite. 'A house in the country…'

'You have a house in the country?'

'No, we don't. Not yet. But we will. London, you
know, is no place to bring up a child.'

'You'd leave the fast lane of London for us?'

'Such a sacrifice, I know,' he murmured lazily. 'And
of course, sacrifices as great as that deserve their reward.'

Marie chuckled. 'They do, don't they?'

'I shall be claiming mine just as soon as we're somewhere private.'

How wonderful, she thought, to have finally come
home.

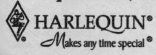

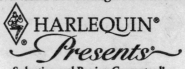

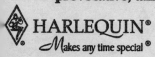

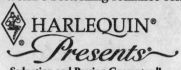

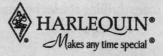

Harlequin is proud to have published
more than 75 novels by

Emma Darcy

Award-
winning Australian
author **Emma Darcy** is a
unique voice in Harlequin
Presents®. Her compelling, sexy,
intensely emotional novels have
gripped the imagination of readers
around the globe, and she's sold
nearly 60 million books
worldwide.

Praise for Emma Darcy:

"Emma Darcy delivers a spicy love story...a fiery conflict
and a hot sensuality."

"Emma Darcy creates a strong emotional premise
and a sizzling sensuality."

"Emma Darcy pulls no punches."

"With exciting scenes, vibrant characters and a layered story line,
Emma Darcy dishes up a spicy reading experience."

—*Romantic Times Magazine*

**Look out for more thrilling stories by Emma Darcy,
coming soon in**